The Memory Thieves

By Diane Ryder

How to Help a Loved One with Dementia, without Losing Your Mind

This book is dedicated to the memory of the earthly teachers and guides of my life: Rev. A.N. Hinrichsen; Miss Jeannette Skidmore; Mr. Otis House; Mr. Clarence Boyle; Jessie Jackson Licklider; Nellie Rae Cuffman; "Grandma" Bertha McKee; Mom and Dad; and to Mary Lou Traucht. These amazing people inspired me, corrected me, taught me, and gave me the skills to become the person, and writer, that I am. God Bless You All.

Based on a True Story

"Well, for cryin' out loud..."

------Lois Licklider Cuffman

1919-2019

Prologue

The Memory Thieves

Mentor, Ohio

July 16, 1974

8:14 p.m.

Mom and Dad knew right away that something was amiss. They didn't have to see the wide-open back door to the house, or the shredded screen on the back window. Sandy told them all they needed to know.

In the back seat, Sandy started whining as soon as they pulled into the driveway.

"What's the matter, Sandy?" Mom asked, twisting in her shotgun seat to face Sandy in the back seat, not really expecting an answer. But when she turned her head for a better look, she could see the hair standing upright, from the top of Sandy's brown head to the white tip of her tail, which, for once, was not wagging. The dog appeared to be frowning, her brow wrinkled and her nose in the air, sniffing.

Then Sandy did something she almost never did. She let out a menacing growl from deep in her throat.

When Dad stopped the car next to the back door, he saw that it was wide open. He was absolutely sure he had locked it tightly when they had left the house six hours earlier.

Mom got out and opened the back car door to let Sandy out. Sandy put on her brakes, whimpered, and refused to leave the car.

"Mother, go next door and call the police," Dad ordered, forcing his voice to be a lot calmer than he felt. "I think we've had a break-in."

Mom squealed in fright, but Dad waved his hand sideways, signaling her to be quiet.

Mentor was a quiet town, and tree-lined Madison Street was its quietest neighborhood, even long after the police chief moved away from the street. Most people never bothered to lock their doors, even when they went on vacation. Dad, of course, was the exception. He must have decided somewhere along the line that if high security was good enough for Fort Knox, it was good enough for him, and it doesn't do any harm to lock the doors. Better safe than sorry.

Leaving Sandy whimpering in the back seat, Mom dashed over to Mrs. Thompson's house next door to use the phone, as Dad fumbled under the car's front seat for the Louisville Slugger baseball bat he always kept there. He knew better than to enter the house with the burglars possibly still in there. Standing at the bottom of the back stairs, he assumed the position of a right-handed slugger, just in case whoever it was tried to escape out the back door.

Mom was soon back, with Mrs. Thompson in tow. The old lady, God bless her, was wielding a paring knife from her kitchen, wiping it on her apron as she ran.

"Must'a been kids, although I didn't see or hear nothin'." Mrs. Thompson opined, as Dad shushed her.

"Be quiet; someone may still be in there," he whispered in the direction of the ladies, his eyes still riveted to the damaged back door. Mom and Mrs. Thompson crouched behind him, Mrs. Thompson still brandishing her deadly weapon.

"Maybe if we let Sandy out, she can run into the house and chase them," Mom offered.

But Sandy, watching intently from the safety of the back seat, was having none of it. Mom could almost see the beagle shaking her furry head. Not this dog, Kemo-sabe, huh uh, no way Jose, she seemed to say.

Ten sloth-like minutes crawled by as the trio waited frantically for police to arrive. For years later, as she related the break-in story multiple times, Mom insisted it took them a half hour, then an hour, then two hours, to arrive. The response time increased as time went on.

The Mentor police determined that, indeed, it had probably been kids, looking for quick cash to buy cigarettes and beer. After they determined that none of the miscreants remained in the house, police escorted Mom and Dad inside to find out what was missing, as Mrs. Thompson went back home to call my brother Gary, my brother Ken, then me; the oldest, but a girl and thus less useful and more inclined to be too emotional in an emergency.

We all reached Mom and Dad's house within a half hour, from our separate homes twenty miles in each direction. The police had already dusted for fingerprints, shot a few half-hearted photos, and had already gone on to their next call.

When we hurried into the kitchen, a worn, very tired broom and dust pan leaned against the overflowing kitchen trash can. Both of our parents were seated at the table, Dad looking pale and clammy; Mom with her head in her hands, sobbing.

"The little stinkers," Dad said. "They slit open a screen on the back window, climbed in, and lighted matches to see with as they went through everything. They dropped the used matches everywhere as they ransacked everything. It's a miracle they didn't start a fire as they went.

"We don't keep much cash in the house, but they broke open Ken's old piggy bank, found the change we keep by the door for the paper boy, and they found my secret $50 bill I keep in my sock drawer for emergencies. All in all, we figure they got about $80."

"Thank God no one was hurt," I said, relieved.

"But that wasn't all," Dad said, his shoulders drooping as he let out his breath.

9

Mom wailed and blew her nose loudly.

"They got my Grandma's pearl necklace, the one she, Mom, you, and I all wore on our wedding days," Mom said between sobs, her voice struggling for air. "And the cocktail ring Dad gave me on our 25th anniversary."

Dad looked as though he was also going to cry.

"And they got my roll of invasion money, my short snort, from the War," he whispered, his voice shaky.

It was customary for GI's to form collections of paper currency from each place they visited during World War II. Dad's roll was quite extensive, from many of the Pacific Islands where he had served. Several of them were autographed by buddies he had served with, some of whom never made it home. The bills were taped together with yellowing cellophane tape, rolled up lovingly, and carefully kept in a hard plastic travel case designed for a bar of soap. Dad kept it in the very back of his underwear drawer, and only took it out on the most special occasions. We'd never been allowed to touch it, only to stare at it in awe, respecting the fact that it represented almost four years of Dad's life back in The War's long ago past.

Gone. His prized possession. I fought back tears at the thought that these items, while not very valuable in terms of money, were priceless to Mom and Dad. Irreplaceable because they represented memories dear to them.

Within hours, police arrested four neighborhood kids, based on their use of matches to light their way through Mom and Dad's house. The boys had done this many times before, and were well known to local law enforcement. The money was long gone, and, unfortunately, so were Mom and Dad's precious heirlooms, undoubtedly sold for a little bit of cash. The boys were vague about what they had done with the items, and could not, or would not, name the person who bought them; just that they had unloaded them on a street corner somewhere on the East Side of Cleveland.

Dad never gave up hope of finding his money roll, but as the years went by, it became less and less likely that it would turn up. And when my oldest daughter got married many years later, Mom wept when she thought of the little pearl necklace in its velvet lined box, lost in that long-ago burglary, that she could not pass down to another generation.

Precious memories treasured, now lost forever.

Chapter One

"WHERE IS DAD?"

Mentor, Ohio

September 9, 2006

12:30 a.m.

We still have a landline for some reason. It's a nuisance, with all the telemarketers eager to share with us ways to save money on our credit cards, or informing us that we won the trip of a lifetime to Jamaica, or some other nonsense. All I can tell you is: I can testify that The Do Not Call List doesn't work.

We'd like to get rid of the old phone, but for some strange reason, it costs too much money to discontinue it. At least, that's what the bandits at the cable company tell us. And you never know when we will need it in an emergency. So, it stays, in the living room, and an extension right next to the bed.

That's what gave me the first indication that there was something wrong.

Late one night, the landline rang, waking us suddenly with a rude interruption. Since the phone is on my night stand, it's up to me to make the ringing stop. Either I can pull the darned thing out of the wall and pitch it across the room, or I can answer it. Ignoring it is not an option.

Our kids are long grown and gone, so a phone call after midnight can be either some drunk misdialing from a party, the grandchild-in-jail scam, or someone close to us is in the hospital.

I felt in the dark for the stupid phone, picked up the receiver, and growled my annoyance.

"Diane? Is that you?" came Mom's frantic voice, breathing loudly in-and-out. Who else would it be?

"Are you okay?" I asked, instantly awake but my voice still fuzzy, as Ed, beside me, sat up and turned on his bedside lamp, temporarily blinding both of us. The clock on the nightstand read 12:35.

"Diane, I don't know what to do. Your Dad's not home. It's not like him to be out this late without calling, and I don't know what to do. Should I call the police? I woke up and he wasn't there. I searched the whole house and called his name, but nothing. I'm afraid something terrible has happened to him. I'm really scared. He's never done this before."

Uh oh.

I tried to remain calm, as Ed asked if everything was okay, knowing full well from my facial expression that it wasn't. I shook my head at Ed, took a deep breath so the panic in my voice wouldn't show, and thought of the best way to answer her, as gently as possible.

"Mom, Dad passed away four years ago."

I could hear her drop the phone as a terrible strangled sound came from the other end. It morphed into a heart-wrenching wail. I motioned to Ed to get dressed, as I got out of bed and looked frantically around the room for my clothes.

"Mom? Pick up the phone! Ed and I will be right over!"

We live forty-five minutes away when there is no traffic. I thought of calling Danielle Thompson Morrow, Mom's next door neighbor and daughter of the late Mrs. Thompson, but thought better of it. No sense in rousing her unnecessarily, although I wasn't completely sure that it wasn't necessary.

I thought of my brother Gary, the last of my siblings, who lived fifteen minutes from Mom. He worked second shift, so he would probably still be up. I told Ed what was happening, as I waited for Mom to pick up the phone. I could hear gurgling sounds from a distance.

Ed picked up his cell phone and dialed Gary, who said he'd go over there right away. That gave me some relief as I continued to yell into the phone for Mom to pick up. Her noises had changed to deep, convulsive sobs.

All the way there, with Ed driving as fast as he could, I prayed that God would watch over Mom till we got there. She was always the Strong One in the family. She had survived losing her family farm to the Dust Bowl, the Great Depression, World War II, nursing both of her parents, and the loss of her husband and three of her children. She was tough as nails, with the memory of an elephant and the proud, pig-headed stubbornness of a Missouri mule.

She was the one member of the family who could always answer the burning questions, "What was Uncle Arthur's dog's name? Who wrote 'Tale of Two Cities'? Who played Louie in 'Casablanca'? How old was Aunt Mattie when she died?"

She would have been great on "Jeopardy," or in a Trivial Pursuits tournament.

It wasn't like Mom to forget the fact that her beloved husband of 56 years had died of cancer four years before, despite all of her best efforts to keep him alive.

I kept trying Mom's landline number on my cell as we drove, but just got a continuous busy signal. I went into Parent Mode, visualizing any number of tragic scenarios. She could have fallen down the stairs, had a heart attack, run outside in her nightgown and gotten hit by a truck. Ed told me to calm down.

"No point in working yourself up until we know what we're dealing with," he said. "You don't want your blood pressure to spike."

When we pulled into Mom's driveway, the outside lights illuminated Gary's truck in the driveway, but no police cars or ambulances. I started to breathe.

I noticed that the outer door now had a small panel of broken glass where Gary had knocked it out. We had told Mom thousands of times not to lock the outer storm door every night, in case a night-time emergency would necessitate our using our keys to get into the house through the main door. Mom had always said, "Don't worry about it. If there's ever an emergency, I'll just come downstairs and let you in."

Both Mom and Dad believed in locking everything up at night, especially after the break-in they had experienced in 1974. Neighborhood kids had sliced a screen, crawled in, and rifled the entire house for cash. They had taken the coins from Ken's old piggy bank, Dad's emergency $50 bill from beneath the paper liner of his underwear drawer, a few irreplaceable family heirlooms, and had generally made a mess of the house. Mom and Dad had never felt safe in their own home, ever again.

My brother Gary met us in the kitchen, illuminated only by one light over Mom's ancient stove. He looked a lot calmer than I, and for some reason that irritated me. Gary had inherited Dad's Scottish stoic gene, while I always had to work hard at being calm.

"Relax," my younger brother said, placing his hand on my shoulder in reassurance. Easy for him to say.

"I found Mom sound asleep when I got here about 20 minutes ago," Gary continued. "Apparently she got back into bed and cried herself to sleep. She seems fine. I don't think we should wake her. We should all go home and check on her in the morning."

I shook my head. "No, I'll stay here with her until she wakes up," I said.

Ed and Gary overruled that idea.

"Think about it," Ed said. "When she gets up in the morning, she'll be startled to find you here. I bet she won't remember this at all."

"But what if she does?" I retorted, annoyed at the whine in my voice. "I'll feel better making sure she is okay."

"No," Ed insisted. "We all need to go home. You can call or even drive over first thing in the morning. You need to calm down and get some sleep. We'll go home and you can take a sleeping pill if you need it. As for me, an Irish whiskey is calling my name when we get home. It's been quite a night."

Of course, pill or not, I tossed and turned all night, barely dozing here and there. Mom had always been the strong one of the family. After all, she was just 11 years old when she had watched all of her family's possessions, from cultivators to washboards to skillets to plow mules, auctioned off one by one, including her family's third generation 160 acre farm back in Missouri. A family's history and treasured memories gone, snatched away with the finality of the auctioneer's gavel.

The family had barely survived four crop failures, the after result of the Dust Bowl. Four years of the traitorous land, that had sustained three generations since the 1840s, refusing to yield more than a skimpy few, anemic vegetables---not enough to feed the farmer parents, six kids, and a grandchild.

Grandma had supplemented the family's meager diet by wading into Bowen's Creek every morning, fishing pole in hand, to catch catfish, which she would clean and fry for their supper every night.

For the rest of her life, Mom couldn't stand the smell of fish cooking, or the sight of the ugly fish with the whiskers, gaping mouths, and perpetual frowns.

At the age of 11, Mom had left everything she had ever known or cherished, including her school, all of her cousins, and her childhood friends, and had started her life over in Ohio, which was a huge culture shock. She had endured constant teasing about her homemade country clothes and her Missouri drawl. But with determination, she not only had survived, she had thrived.

Mom had started and run her own business, a beauty salon, at a time when women owning businesses was discouraged, and rare. She fell in love with a G.I who wrote great letters, and when he finally returned from the War, she had been engaged for over a year to a man she had never held or kissed.

She had married just three weeks after her father's death from leukemia, in a quiet ceremony her dying Pop had insisted they not delay. She and Dad had built their own house, board by board, from the ground up and had lived there for seven decades.

She had lost one baby, a boy, to miscarriage and had buried two other sons; one at nine weeks, and the other at age 37. She had endured an undiagnosed, decades-long battle with mental illness. Then she had lost the love of her life at age 82.

These thoughts, and many of their cousins, whirled and zoomed around through my head, crowding out any chance of sleep. Mom had always been the rational one---the rock of our household. She had amazed everyone with her strength and survival instincts when Dad, the center of her universe for 56 years, had succumbed to esophageal cancer in 2002.

Once or twice a week for the last four years, Mom and I would go out to lunch, following a morning of errands and visiting one or two of Dad's eight favorite banks, as we worked to consolidate his 31 different accounts.

After he had retired, Dad had devoted his time and considerable financial talents to the challenge of bringing in a steady income and saving as much money as he could for their eventual medical and physical needs. Always up for a challenge, he had developed a complicated, but efficient, system of investments, certificates of deposit, T-bills, individual retirement accounts, mutual funds, stocks, and, of course, Social Security income, to ensure that pretty much every day a check from one source or another would arrive in their mailbox. That was enough to support them if they were frugal. Dad could have written a book on how to pinch pennies. He was, after all, half Scottish.

Dad, the penultimate engineer, loved a challenge, and the more difficult the challenge, the more he poured himself into it. He was usually successful, maybe not at the first try, but he'd keep at it until he was satisfied. So it was with his system. He fine-tuned it into a comfortable, steady, moderate income, all perfectly safe and legal.

The problem was, I didn't inherit even one financial wizard gene. Oh, I liked money as much as everyone else, but my expertise tended to be more on the spending end. Dad would chuckle and shake his head at me. "Are you sure you're my daughter?" he'd gently jab, as he'd lend me ten bucks for gas.

Which bought a full tank back in those days.

So within a few months of his passing, it became very clear that Mom and I were not equipped to understand his system. We traveled from bank to bank, at first working with Dad's favorite bank officials, whom we had always teasingly referred to as Dad's "girlfriends."

One day, a year after Dad's passing, and Mom and I had visited four of Dad's banks to negotiate new rates on CDs that had matured, I told Mom over lunch, "Look, I can't keep my own checkbook straight. There is no way that either one of us can keep track of Dad's system. It's too complicated, and I'm afraid I'll screw it up and lose your money. I think it's time that we eliminate some of these banks and consolidate all these accounts."

Mom took a sip of her Sprite, thought for a moment, and nodded.

"You're probably right," she said. "I think Dad would want us to manage this without going crazy. He'd understand."

Concessions of any sort were not in her realm. I was surprised, and relieved, that she saw the logic. Either that, or she was tired of me dragging her from bank to bank every few days.

So, over the next several years, Mom chose her three favorite banks, mainly because of the ladies Dad had dealt with for decades. As the dozens of CDs would come due, every few months, we would cash them out and place them in one of three consolidated accounts, all in the name of Mom, Gary, and me.

"Why don't we do it that way?" Mom suggested. "After all, my new will leaves everything equally to you and Gary. That way, if something happened to one of us, the others would share everything equally."

Our timing was serendipitous, for once, because the interest rates were starting to slide, and the CDs that Dad had arranged at 8 percent interest now were yielding only two or three.

Mom seemed to appreciate the new plan, as her accounts in three banks grew and we gradually needed to stop at fewer and fewer banks every week. We arranged for a safe deposit box in her favorite bank in all three names, and placed in it a watch, Dad's wedding ring, some of Mom's best jewelry, their birth certificates and their 1946 marriage license, and other valuables we would be devastated to lose. We also put in 35 mm slides Dad had painstakingly made of the interior of their house. Dad left nothing to chance. Hope for the best, but prepare for the worst.

After the theft of some precious heirlooms in the 1974 break-in, it made sense to keep the few pieces left in a safe deposit box.

It's amazing the clarity of thought when sleep is being elusive.

I must have finally fallen asleep as the bedroom window showed a glimmering promise of sunrise. I woke about 9 a.m., and as I poured my first cup of coffee before deciding what to do, the phone rang, and the caller ID showed Mom's phone number since 1955. Time to find out what she remembered of last night's events.

"Hello?" Mom asked.

"How are you doing?" I ventured.

"Just fine," she said. "I just got up about fifteen minutes ago. I must have been very tired."

No mention of the events of last night.

"Did you sleep okay?"

"Yes," she said. "I think I must have had had some pretty wild dreams, but I don't remember them."

Whew. Bullet dodged. She must have had a very realistic dream about Dad, and was still semi-asleep when she had called me. I'm so glad she didn't encounter me on her couch when she got up. That would only have alarmed her. Ed and Gary had been right, darn it.

"What are your plans for today?" I asked.

"I'm havin' my breakfast right now. Grapefruit and cereal. Would you believe that your brother's here to fix a broken pane in the storm door? He said he thinks the lawn service must have kicked up a stone when they mowed yesterday. I don't know why I didn't notice it when I locked up last night. "

Bless Gary's quick thinking.

"Then I thought I'd go to the store," Mom said. "I need a few things."

"Do you want me to come and take you?" Our semi-weekly bank trips usually included a stop at her favorite grocery store.

"No, don't bother. I drive the back roads, and the car knows the way to the store and back."

Mom insisted on driving Dad's ancient boat, a 1986 top-of-the-line, Cartier edition, silver Lincoln Town Car. I think she considered it a tangible link to Dad. Concerned about her eyesight and ability to drive, I had gone with her three weeks before to see how well she would do. She handled that Lincoln, which had taken them on more than 275,000 miles of adventures over the years, like a pro. It barely fit into the garage, but she drove it in and out perfectly every time without hesitation, and stopped it when her windshield touched the tennis ball that Dad had suspended from the garage rafters to mark the right spot to park. Dad always had a practical, logical solution to every problem. Once an engineer, always an engineer. Problem solving was his obsession.

Using the back roads through her neighborhood and the adjacent development, intrepid Mom could go to the store or the post office without ever using the main road. She was very careful, and her eyesight, repaired with cataract surgery ten years before, was sharper than mine.

I silently wondered how much longer she would be able to drive, and how on earth I would get her to relinquish her precious driver's license when the time came. We made plans for an errands day later in the week, and said goodbye. Whew. Another crisis averted. Thanks, Dad.

Chapter Two

Mentor, Ohio

September 17, 2008

"IT WAS JUST A LITTLE FIRE"

Our lives settled back into a comfortable routine, with a gradual but steady increase in my supervision of Mom, with calls to her every morning, and from Mom to me every night to check in before her 8 p.m. bedtime. Twice a week, or more if needed, I would spend half a day taking her to doctor or dentist appointments, picking up her prescriptions from Wal-Mart, and taking her to the bank. I tried to make them fun, adding lunch in a new restaurant or sharing a sandwich in one of the local parks.

Broaching a sensitive subject with Mom was always tricky. She had to believe that any decision she made was based on her own original thought or idea, and that was easier said than done.

Over lunch one Wednesday, I got up the courage to ask, "How much longer to you plan to drive?"

"Why? Am I becoming a bad driver?" she bristled. I could see her spine stiffen in indignation as she glared at me.

"No, not at all; you've always been an excellent driver. I was just wondering if you've thought about it at all."

"Well, yes, as a matter of fact, I have," she sniffed, as she sprinkled salt on her sandwich. Mom salted everything that went into her mouth. Salad, soup, grapefruit, cantaloupe, tomatoes, watermelon, her favorite corn on the cob. She never went anywhere without a travel salt shaker or packet of salt in her purse.

"As you know, I turn 89 this November," she said. "I know that when I turn 90, I'll have to take an eye test and a road test in order to renew my license. I don't want to do that. I'll be too nervous and will probably flub it. So, instead of risking failing, I have decided to give up driving on my 90th birthday. What do you think of that?"

Whew.

I took a slow bite of my sandwich to stall, then chose my words carefully, shielding my relief as best I could.

"That sounds reasonable," I ventured, nodding. I took another bite of my peanut butter and jelly sandwich, sans salt, and tried to look thoughtful to hide my relief.

"By that time the car will be 28 years old, which is pretty old for a car, even one of ours," she said, finishing her sandwich and opening a small bottle of Sprite. "Maybe it's time for both the car and me to retire from driving."

When Dad first was diagnosed with cancer, Mom had to take over driving his pride and joy, his silver Lincoln Town Car, with 275,000 miles that we knew of. The odometer had broken years ago.

That car had been everywhere: first taking Dad to work every day, vacations, family visits, winter trips to Florida, annual reunions of Dad's World War II group, the Grey Geese, visits to every state capital (except maybe Juneau and Honolulu), and almost every bird sanctuary, state and national park that they knew or had heard about. Dad's considerable mechanical skills had kept the car in tip-top shape, including the driver's side mirror fastened with a coat hanger and the sawed-off broomstick he used to keep the hood open when he was working on the engine. His loving care had kept it shiny and dirt-free, with no visible scratches or dings.

Dad could have afforded a newer, more energy efficient, smaller car, but he would never give up his Lincoln. It barely fit into the garage, but he hung a tennis ball from the rafters in just the right position, announcing when it was time to stop when he drove it in. And just in case, he also had blocks positioned in the floor to stop the car from hitting the interior wall. Dad left nothing to chance.

Mom was contented to leave the driving to Dad, but when she had to drive, she handled that massive vehicle expertly. Her cataracts had been removed in 1998, which sharpened her eyesight to predatory bird status. Dad actually teased her by calling her "Ol' Eagle Eye."

But she, and the Lincoln, which was also part of the family, weren't getting any younger.

"I just use the backroads mostly," Mom explained. "I can get to the store, and back, that way. I don't like driving on the main roads if I can help it, and not on the freeway anymore. Everybody's in such a hurry. And I won't drive at night, when all the drunks are on the roads."

Lunch was over, and so was the topic of conversation, apparently. We packed up our picnic and headed for the car.

Late one September day, Mom called, a little earlier than usual. I should have suspected that something was amiss.

"Just checking in," she purred, her voice almost musical. Something was up.

 "I think I'll turn in early tonight."

"Mom, it's 5:30," I said. "I've just started making dinner."

"Oh? What are you making?"

"Your chicken and rice casserole. The one with cream of chicken soup."

"Sounds good. Dad always liked it. Save some for me, will you? I am pretty tired tonight. I had a long day."

"How so?" I asked, feeling the hair on the back of my neck stand at attention.

"Well, I ran some errands and noticed that the car was running low on gas."

"Mom, I just filled your tank last week," I told her. "Have you been driving a lot the last few days?"

"No, I haven't, but the needle showed less than three-fourths full, and I don't want to run out, so after I got my groceries, I went to the gas station. I decided to pump the gas on my own, the way you showed me. In my day, they came out and pumped your gas for you, checked your oil, and even washed your windows, all free of charge." She added a sigh for good measure.

"I know. I remember those days," I said. "So were you able to fill the tank?"

"Oh, yes, but the funniest thing happened. The car caught on fire right there at the gas pump." She added a chuckle for good measure.

"WHAT?!!!!" I dropped the mixing spoon on the floor with a clatter and splatter of soup and rice.

"Oh, it was fine," she said. "They came right out in a hurry and put it out. They were very nice about it."

"Wait! What happened! Where was the fire?"

"I told you," she said in her patient-parent voice. "At the gas pump."

"NO! WHERE WAS IT ON THE CAR?"

"You don't have to raise your voice with me, young lady. I'm not deaf. It was in the back, somewhere around the back wheel," Mom replied. "It was only a little fire. They didn't even need to call the fire department, thank goodness. That would have been embarrassing. They put it out with a fire extinguisher. They got it out right away before any damage was done. They were very nice about it."

"So what did you do then?"

"I thanked them, got in the car, and drove home."

"Mom! The car was probably not safe to drive!"

"Well, I don't live far. It was fine. Much ado about nothing. All's well that ends well."

I tried to sound a lot calmer than I felt. I told her to go to bed, said a hasty goodnight, and hung up. I had Gary on speed-dial.

"Holy crap," my brother said. "Okay, I'll go over there in the morning and take the car over to Ernie's. He'll get it up on the lift and we'll give it a thorough going-over. But chances are, the wiring's all screwed up and rotted out. I'm surprised she was able to get it home."

By the next afternoon, the verdict, according to family mechanic Ernie, and my brother concurring, was that the entire underside of the car was rusted and rotted, and the electrical wires were all shot. Driving the car was dangerous, and repairing it was out of the question. The Lincoln, Dad's pride for more than two decades, was for all purposes dead. Driving it the four miles from the repair shop back to Mom's was not an option. Ernie said it was a miracle that

Mom had gotten it home safely, and that Gary had driven it the four miles to the mechanic's garage without incident.

"An angel was watching over you," Ernie opined, nodding in agreement with his diagnosis. "Just leave it here until you can junk it."

So I drove out there to pick Gary up. We stopped for coffee on our way back to Mom's, to discuss our options.

"Mom will be devastated; she was planning to drive for another few months. She will hate losing her independence," I told Gary.

"So our choices are finding her a car she can drive, or you and I taking turns driving her everywhere she needs to go," he said. "Maybe find her a small Buick or something she can handle easily."

I shook my head. "You know Mom. She was used to the Lincoln. She could handle it easily and knew all of its quirks. She won't be able to get used to a different car at this stage of her life."

"I have an idea," he said. "Why don't we try to find another Lincoln of the same age?"

"Gary, where are we going to find a 27-year-old, top-of-the-line, silver Lincoln Town Car in good condition?"

"I'll ask around," he said. "And maybe we can find one on Craig's List. You can pretty much find anything there. And the Lincolns of that era lasted forever. I still see a lot of them on the road."

"Until they catch fire," I pointed out.

Sure enough, four days later I spotted a listing and photo of a 1986 Lincoln Town Car for sale two towns over, for $1,100. I made an appointment to go see it, and made arrangements for Gary to go with me.

"I think you're foolish," Ed said. "Buying her something she'll never drive. And it's probably a chop shop. Make sure the car has a legitimate title. I just hope you don't regret doing this."

The address was a mechanic's garage behind a small split level home in a rural neighborhood. Red flags seem to go up in my head as we drove back to the workshop, where three scary-looking, ponytailed, tattooed and whiskered men in overalls were working on a variety of old cars.

We spotted the car immediately. It was a Lincoln Town Car, all right, but it was rather plain, charcoal grey, and not at all shiny. But how many 1986 Lincoln Town Cars were available for sale right now, just when we needed to find one?

The shop owner, a man named Dwayne, shook our hands and said, "Ain't she a beauty? I hate to sell her, because she only has 64,000 miles, and I've been using her myself. She runs perfectly, but I need to clear out some of my stock of cars back here."

The car looked a little tired to have only 64,000 miles, so I asked Gary to look it over carefully and tell me whether he thought the guy was telling the truth. Dwayne seemed a little too sincere, almost eager. Red flags were going Ding, Ding, Ding all over the place.

The car started right up, as Gary crawled underneath to inspect the undercarriage. After several minutes, he rolled out from underneath and opened the hood to get a close look at the engine.

"See how clean she is?" Dwayne said. "I just tuned her up, and put in new plugs. The brakes are good and the tires have plenty of tread."

"What's the history of the car?" I asked.

"It's only had one owner, a minister from Euclid," Dwayne said. "He had some health issues and couldn't drive anymore."

Ding. Ding. Ding.

"Listen, Dwayne, we need a safe, dependable car for our 89-year-old mother, who is used to driving an '86 town car. Can you guarantee this car will be safe for her? Would you allow your mother to drive it?" I asked.

"My own mom has driven this, lots of times," Dwayne said. "I wouldn't hesitate to put an old lady behind the wheel of this baby. And I don't always do this, but if your mom doesn't like the car, I'll take it back and give you a refund. This car is easy to sell."

Gary and I took turns driving it around the neighborhood. It handled well, but the shifting was a little stiff. I wondered whether Mom would have the strength to shift it on the column. But the engine ran smoothly and the ride was comfortable and quiet.

After we drove it, Gary took me aside, and said the car looked in excellent condition overall, but he somehow doubted the mileage was quite as low as Dwayne said.

"It's clean, no oil leaking anywhere, and the tires look good," Gary said. "The only thing is, it has cloth seats instead of leather, and none of the bells and whistles that Dad's car had. But I think Mom could drive this for the few months she has left to drive. And it's a good price."

We decided that Dad would have approved of our plan, regardless of the red flags, which seemed to have vanished somehow.

We negotiated the price down to $1,000, and I wrote out a check. Dwayne gave me a handwritten note guaranteeing that we could return the car within 7 days for a full refund.

"There is a little problem with the title," Dwayne said, as the red flags went back up again. "Oh, don't worry. I have a clear title. But I am having a complication with the county over some back taxes they say I owe. I have a friend at the BMV who will take care of transferring the title and getting you plates. Her name is Denise and she'll take care of everything. It'll all be legal, I swear. You'll just need to meet me there, say in an hour."

So, despite the red flags, and the fact that every instinct I had screamed at me to run away from this deal, I did meet Dwayne at a BMV about 20 miles away, and a young woman with too much hair and several piercings in inappropriate places took care of whatever problem it was, Dwayne gave her an envelope, and I drove away with the (hopefully) legitimate title and license plates.

I drove to Mom's, where Gary sat in the driveway with the "new" Lincoln. He found one of Dad's screwdrivers in his old leather tool belt hanging on a peg in the garage, and put on the new plates. We both went into the house and announced to Mom that we had a surprise for her. She looked out the window, overlooking the driveway, and the expression of total disbelief on her face was priceless.

"Whose car is that?" she asked. "It looks a little like Dad's."

Gary handed her the keys.

"It's yours," I told her. "We found a replacement as close to Dad's as we could, something you already know how to drive."

She was dumbfounded.

"I can't believe you found one," Mom said, as we helped her outside and she circled the outside of her new car. "It's not the same, of course, but it's a lot like it."

Gary opened the driver's side door for her. She got in, started it up, and with a grin, put it into gear.

"It's a little stiff, but I think I can manage," she said. With Gary next to her, and me in the back seat, she eased it once around the block and pulled it back into the driveway without any hesitation.

"I can't believe you kids did this for me," she said, her voice shaky with emotion. "I figured my driving days were over when Dad's car died. I don't know how much longer I'll be driving, but this is great for now. Thank you!"

Mom drove the new-old Lincoln for about two months, mostly to the grocery store, never in snow, ice, or rain, and always on the back roads. One day in November, two weeks before her 90th birthday, she called me to describe her ordeal at the grocery store, when she couldn't find her car keys after she loaded her groceries.

She spent an hour backtracking through the store, searching frantically for her keys in the produce section, the freezers, and the dairy case. She finally stopped at the customer service desk, hoping someone had found them and turned them in. She emptied her purse and her pockets, her panic rising.

Barb, the assistant manager who always looked out for Mom at the store, sent two stock boys out to search the Lincoln. After ten minutes, one of them located the keys that had fallen between the seats. Mom, still shaking, was in no condition to drive, so one of them drove the mile to her home, while the other followed in his personal car. They brought Mom and her groceries into the house, and one of them put everything away while the other settled Mom into her chair and gave her a glass of water.

Mom never drove again. One gloomy day in early December, Gary and I watched as a charity picked up the Lincoln and drove it away, ending a 70-year chapter in Mom's independence.

Chapter Three

"I Won a Car!"

May 10, 2010

Early one spring morning, Mom called, breathless with excitement.

"Guess what? I won a new car!" she squealed. "What's a Kia?"

"It's a Korean car," I told her.

"Well, just so it's not Japanese," Mom retorted. "Your Dad fought the Japs, and he would never tolerate anyone in our family having a Japanese car."

"How do you know you won?" I asked, completely skeptical.

"I got this notice in the mail, with my name in big letters at the top," Mom panted. "It had a car key attached to it, and said I should come in and claim my new car. Isn't that wonderful? I've never won anything big in my life, except that one time I won $15 worth of groceries. Fed the family for a week. And now a car? I finally got lucky!"

I hated to be the bearer of bad news, but there was no one else in the room, so it was up to me, the designated family bubble burster.

"Mom, I got one too, and so did just about everybody in Northeast Ohio," I told her, as gently as I could.

"Really?" Mom asked. "How can they afford to give a new car to everybody?"

"It's an ad, Mom," I said. "I'm sorry. You're supposed to bring the key in and see if it fits. None of them do. The dealership just wants you to go there, look at their cars, and buy one."

I hated breaking her heart like that. Sure enough, I could hear the tears in her voice.

"You mean I don't get a car after all?" she sniffed and blew her nose.

"I'm afraid not," I said. "And you gave up your driver's license when you turned ninety, remember?"'

"Did I?" Mom asked. "Where was I? I don't remember doing that. Dad's old Lincoln is still in the garage, isn't it?"

Oh, boy.

"No, Mom, don't you remember? It caught fire last September and we had to get rid of it. We bought you another one, which you drove for a couple of months till you turned 90. You decided to give up your license then."

"I did? Why would I do a thing like that?"

"It was your decision. You didn't want to take a road test to renew your license when you turned 90. You were afraid you wouldn't pass."

"Oh," she said. "So how do I get my groceries?"

"I come out once or twice a week and take you to the store. We run any other errands you need, and sometimes we go out to lunch too. Don't you remember?"

The sound of muffled sobs coming from the other end of the phone broke my heart.

"So what do I do with this notice I got in the mail?" she whined. "Shame on them for tricking a trusting old lady."

"When you get something in the mail, check the upper right corner. Unless it has a regular stamp on it or says FIRST CLASS, just throw it out. It's an ad."

"Oh, I can't do that," Mom said. "What if it's something important?"

"If it's important, it will have a first class stamp on it. Otherwise it's junk. Just throw it out."

Mom's hesitation at the other end of the line was palpable.

"I know what I'll do," she said at last. "I'll make two piles on the kitchen table, one of important stuff and one of ads and junk mail. You can go over it when you come. I'd hate to throw away anything important."

Okay. That'll work.

When I arrived at Mom's on Wednesday, there were two piles of mail waiting for me at one end of the kitchen table. Mom's worn checkbook sat on top of one small pile, and the other pile looked like ads. I tackled the smaller pile first.

"I don't know how much longer I can manage my bills," Mom said. "It gets harder and harder to balance my checkbook, and I'm always worrying I'll forget to pay one and they'll turn off my gas or lights."

"I can take that over for you whenever you want me to," I assured her.

"I can't figure out the balance," she said. "Every month there's about $1,700 more in my account than I thought there would be. It's almost like somebody is putting money into my account every month."

"Could that be your Social Security?" I asked. "Do you have direct deposit of your Social Security check each month?"

"You mean I get $1,700 from the government EVERY month?" Mom demanded. "When did this start happening?"

"When you turned 65, about 25 years ago," I told her.

"Don't be impertinent with me, Miss Smarty Pants," Mom warned.

41

"It's true. You've been getting Social Security for a long time. Dad did too."

"What???? No wonder our country's so far in debt and going broke," Mom said. "Sending all those checks to people. Socialism, that's what it is."

I picked up an official-looking envelope with "OHIO VALLEY GAS CONSORTIUM" in bold letters in the upper left hand corner, and an address in Marietta, Ohio. It had already been opened, and "SHOW DIANE" printed in block letters in Mom's careful hand in red pencil on the front. I opened it.

"Thank you for choosing Ohio Valley Gas Consortium as your natural gas provider," the cheery letter began.

Huh?

"Mom, did you change your gas supplier recently?" I asked.

"I don't think so," Mom ventured. "At least, I don't remember doing it."

I put the letter in my purse. No need to upset her. I'll call them when I get home.

"So much junk mail," Mom complained. "They all want to take advantage of old ladies."

"When you see they are not marked FIRST CLASS MAIL, with an actual stamp, just throw it away," I told her.

"Oh, I can't do that," Mom said. "What if it's something important? It's hard to tell the difference. Is there any way I can refuse junk mail, like we did with the DO NOT CALL list for the phone. It's terrible how many crooks try to con old people."

I told her that the only way to stop junk mail was to change her mailing address, so the post office wouldn't forward the third class mail.

"That sounds like a good idea," she said.

"Except then your mail wouldn't come here at all," I told her. "We could have your mailing address changed to mine, then I could bring you any cards, bills, or letters when I'd get them. All your first class mail would come to my house, except for the junk mail."

"And what would happen to that?"

"The Post Office would throw it away," I told her.

Mom pondered this for several moments.

"What if you lost one of the bills?" she asked. "Then I'd really be up the crick."

"Well, would you want to give me your checkbook and have me pay all of your bills for you? That way you wouldn't have to worry about missing a payment, or balancing your checkbook," I offered, knowing full well I couldn't balance a checkbook to save my life.

"It's a joint account, in your name and mine, so I can write and sign checks for you," I added, already

43

regretting my offer. This is a huge responsibility. I wasn't sure I was ready for that, but somebody had to handle it, and I didn't see any other hands going up.

"Let me think about it," Mom said. "I'll let you know."

When I arrived home, I took the Ohio Valley letter, and two more, out of my purse. A second letter offered Mom water line insurance, and the third offered to consolidate her credit cards.

She only had two credit cards that I knew of: a Mastercard for emergencies, and Dad's worn old Sears card, unused since he passed away. Mom kept it as a souvenir, along with Dad's driver's license, AARP, and Golden Buckeye cards.

I called Ohio Valley, and a pleasant-sounding woman named Laurene answered the phone, with a businesslike, but very southern Ohio, accent. I explained the situation.

"We get this all the time," Laurene said. "Do you happen to have guardianship, or a power of attorney, for your mom?"

I was relieved that Ed had insisted on updating Mom's will after Dad passed, and establishing a durable power of attorney and health care power of attorney, giving me authority to sign for Mom. She signed all those papers with enthusiasm, and Gary had approved as well.

"Yes, I do," I told her.

"Then we can take care of this easily," Laurene said. "I'll send you a form to sign and return, and your mom's gas provider will revert to the previous company. No problem. Should only take a couple of days."

Problem solved.

Two weeks later, Mom called.

"I have a mound of mail here that you need to go through," she said. "Most of it looks like junk, and everything asks me to make decisions. I'm tired of making decisions. I'm scared I'll make the wrong one. What do you think Dad would want me to do?"

"I think Dad would be distressed to see you worried about mail and bills," I answered. "Have you given any thought to what we talked about, transferring your address here?"

"We did? Does that mean I'm moving in with you?"

God forbid.

"No, it just means that all your mail will come to my house, and there will be no more junk mail," I said.

Mom sighed.

"Let's do it. I trust you," she managed.

So we filled out the form with the post office and I dropped it off the next week. Three days later, Mom called.

"I need you to call the Post Office," she said. "Something's wrong. I'm not getting any mail."

"We had it all transferred to my house, remember, Mom?" I asked.

"Why would I do that?" she asked. "Am I moving in with you?"

Mom told me she had been shoveling the front steps every morning for the mailman, because if they were snowy, he wouldn't stop.

"Maybe that's why I don't get any mail," she said. "I might not have done a very good job of clearing the snow. Somehow it's getting harder to do."

"Mom! Please don't try to shovel snow!" I said, raising my voice. "You could get hurt."

For the next three weeks, Mom would call every day, complaining of no mail. I finally made a little sign: DON'T OPEN THE DOOR. YOUR MAIL IS GOING TO DIANE'S HOUSE. SHE WILL BRING IT TO YOU EVERY WEEK. I posted it on the wall next to the front doorknob.

It took several months until she no longer missed getting mail. After awhile, she no longer asked how her bills were being paid. I made arrangements for direct payment from her account for all of her regular bills, and paid her taxes and insurance bills by check when they arrived.

One summer evening several months later, about 7 p.m., we had just finished dinner when the phone rang.

"Something terrible is going to happen," Mom exclaimed, her breathing heavy. "The electric company is going to turn off my lights."

"No, they aren't, Mom," I tried to reassure her. "Your bills are all paid up to date."

"Well, I got something in the mail from the electric company saying something about buying some kind of line insurance, and I'm afraid they'll shut off my electricity if I don't do it."

"Mom, calm down. You shouldn't have received any mail, but somehow you did. Pick up the envelope and look in the upper right corner. What does it say?"

"THIRD CLASS. BULK RATE."

"Okay, that's an ad. That's junk mail. Read it to me."

Mom read the form letter, which sounded very official, offering Mom insurance on her electric line, something we had already been paying extra for, for decades. Dad had approved it.

"Mom, I don't know why you got it, but it's junk mail. Throw it away."

"I can't!" Mom wailed. "What if they turn off my electricity and I sit here alone in the dark?"

"They won't. I guarantee they won't. Now let me hear you tear it up and throw it away."

"No," Mom insisted. "I'll leave it here on the kitchen table for you to see."

I knew that if she did that, she would be up all night, reading it over and over, worried that she'd be using candles to go to bed at night.

"Mom, you have to tear it up and throw it away, and I have to hear you do it."

"No," Mom whined, and started to cry. "I wish I knew what to do. I wish Dad was here to take care of it."

"You know what to do. TEAR IT UP AND THROW IT AWAY. Either you do it, or I'll drive there myself and do it. Either way, it has to be destroyed, right now, tonight."

"I'd hate for you to drive all this way, by yourself, at night," she whined.

"Then throw it away now, and I won't have to," I said.

"No, I just can't," she whispered.

"Okay, I'll be there in 45 minutes; I'm leaving now," I said, frustrated and angry by this time. What idiot at the post office delivered mail to her house?

"You shouldn't drive at night by yourself," Mom sniffed. "There are drunks on the road at night and it's just not safe."

"THEN TEAR IT UP AND THROW IT AWAY!"

"No."

Ed was watching a baseball game on TV, so I told him my errand and headed out, still steaming. I had gotten ten miles when my cell rang. Mom.

"Are you okay?" Mom asked. "Is Ed with you?"

"No, I left him home. I can handle this on my own," I fumed.

"I hate to have you come all this way by yourself," she said. "How many drunks have you seen on the road so far?"

"None that I know of," I said. "I'll be there in about 20 minutes."

Ten minutes later, the cell rang again. Guess who.

"Why aren't you here yet?" Mom asked. "Are you in a ditch somewhere?"

"No, Mom, everything is fine. Look at the clock. In 10 minutes, I'll be pulling into your driveway."

"I hope you brought your toothbrush and a change of clothes," Mom said. "You should stay here with me overnight so you don't have to worry about the drunks."

As promised, ten minutes later, I pulled into the driveway and tried my best to calm down and pull myself together. I could feel my blood pressure elevating by the minute.

Mom was sitting at the kitchen table, the culprit in her hand. Sure enough. An ad for line insurance.

Angrier than I should have been, I grabbed the offending item, tore it into bits, and put the pieces in my pocket. Mom was horrified.

"You're not going home now, are you?" Mom asked.

"You bet I am," I said. "I want to salvage the rest of the evening. The Indians are on." I kissed her on the cheek to show I wasn't mad at her, just very frustrated. I turned on her TV, set it to the Cleveland Indians game, and got her settled in her back-torturing rocking chair, feet propped up on an ottoman, with a small bowl of M&Ms in her lap.

But before I left, I made another small sign: NEVER PUT MAIL OR ANYTHING ELSE IN THIS MAILBOX! and taped it to the outside of her mailbox.

The next day, I had a pleasant but pointed chat with the postmaster, explaining to her the importance of NOT putting any mail in Mom's mailbox, EVER.

"I'm very sorry," she said. "Our regular carrier was on vacation, and a substitute did it." She promised to block off the mail slot for Mom's address on the route case.

To my relief, Mom eventually stopped checking for mail.

One day several weeks later, during our morning phone call, she said, "Somebody put a sign on my mailbox saying no mail can be put in there. I wondered why I hadn't been getting any mail lately. Now I know. I wonder who would do a thing like that."

Chapter Four

July 20, 2011

"I Can Never Have Curls Again."

Wednesday was usually errand day with Mom. It was my day to check on her, make sure her clothes were clean, she had everything she needed, and was eating regular meals. It was also our time together, out of the house; a time to bond and have some fun.

It was hard to supervise her without her knowledge, but it was important for her to keep some dignity and believe, even if it wasn't true, that she still led an independent life. As time went on, it was increasingly difficult to maintain the illusion, because she found making even the smallest decisions to be daunting.

On this particular sunny Wednesday morning in July, I hoped to find Mom in a good mood. The presence, or absence, of sunlight did a lot to determine her outlook at any given time. Calling her on a grey or rainy day would be a mistake, because she would invariably be the Voice of Doom.

But lucky for both of us, the sun was bright as I walked into her kitchen. She was standing at her powder room sink, just off the kitchen, her right hand holding her ancient curling iron. She was humming her favorite song, "You Are My Sunshine." She didn't notice me, so I kept in the background, contented to watch her for a minute.

As she applied the curling iron to her sparse white fluff, she suddenly frowned and reached a tentative finger to the barrel.

"Hi, Mom. What's up?" I asked, not wanting to startle her.

"I don't know what's wrong with this thing. It's not heating," she said, and handed it to me for verification.

Sure enough. Stone cold. I tried the switch, tried unplugging it and re-plugging it. Nothing.

"I think it's dead," I informed Mom.

"That can't be," she said. "I've only had it twenty or twenty-five years. Dad fixed it with duct tape several times. It always worked great."

"Then it had a good long life," I said solemnly.

She started to wail.

"I can never go out in public again! I'll never have curls again!"

Oh, dear.

"Sure you will, Mom. Don't worry. This is a problem easily solved."

"Is there a repair shop where you can take it?" she asked. "Big Russ was always our repair man for the TV and anything else that Dad couldn't fix by himself. I may still have his number here somewhere."

I didn't have the heart to tell her that Big Russ sold his TV and small appliance repair shop and moved to Florida in 1965, and that no one repairs such things these days, even if they knew how, because everything is made in China to be disposable. She would be horrified to know that we have become a Throw Away Society. She grew up in a time when you fixed it, made do, or did without.

"I'll be right back," I assured Mom.

Drug Mart is right around the corner, in a former A&P. I found a simple curling iron, similar to the old one, saw that it was on clearance for $9.99, and took it in triumph to the cashier. I was back in less than 10 minutes. Easy peasy. Problem solved.

Mom was dumbfounded when I plugged in her new curling iron and it heated up almost immediately.

"What??? You mean all these years I could have had a new one?"

She finished curling her ultra fine, wispy hair, then squinted in the mirror as she applied full matte make-up, Cover Girl #3, carefully smearing it onto the brown spots on her neck. Then she expertly applied her favorite Cherry Kiss lipstick.

"If you ever come here and see that I haven't curled my hair and put on my make-up, you'll know it's time to put me in a home," she said, peering at me from the mirror.

"I'm sure that won't happen for a long time yet," I assured her, with more confidence than I felt. "Don't worry about it."

"I do worry about it," she replied, wrinkling her brow. "I can tell I'm getting more and more forgetful every day. I don't know how much longer I will be able to live by myself. I sure miss Dad. It's no fun living alone."

"We'll cross that bridge when we come to it," I said, with more courage in my words than I felt. "Hopefully that won't be for a long time yet."

I walked over to the heart of Mom's kitchen—the big 1964 era table, formica-topped, with brass legs and trim. Lots of birthdays, Thanksgivings, Christmases, and New Year's Eve card games held around that table over a half century.

The table had one bare spot for Mom to sit and have her meals, when she wasn't eating them off a tray table in front of the TV, that is. The rest of the space was crammed with a partially completed jigsaw puzzle of a rural scene in the Fall, newspapers, books of partially completed crossword puzzles, photos of the grandkids and great-grandkids, and two very dry, long-dead plants.

Hmm. Never noticed that before. Mom loved her plants, watering and trimming them carefully, cooing to them, and generally treating them like babies. The ones in the dining room had been her pride for as long as I could remember, especially her massive rope plant, probably close to a century old, wound around and around a small trellis Dad had made for it when I was maybe 12. That took up one whole window. The other window had a spider plant, laden with "babies," and her beloved Christmas cactus. Curious, I walked into the dining room. My heart sank.

All dry brown corpses, forgotten and forlorn. In my weekly and twice-weekly trips to see Mom, I hadn't noticed the plants. Guilt stabbed me like a tetanus shot.

Now, the only plants that survive under my care are silk, but even I know that plants need regular water. Poor things. I found Mom's battered plastic watering can, filled it up at the sink, and quietly poured water on the plants, in the slight chance they were not dead-dead, just comatose.

Mom, eating her Quaker Oat Squares in the kitchen, sat with her back to me, oblivious to the carnage I was witnessing in the adjoining room.

I gave the plants another soaking for good measure, then put the watering can back in her broom closet. I decided to say nothing.

I asked Mom if she was ready to go to the store. Still munching her cereal, she reached over to one of the piles on the table and held up a long paper tape. She kept a running shopping list on a roll of adding machine paper mounted on a wooden dowel. The miniature butcher block paper had been a hand-crafted gift from a friend many years ago. It was becoming increasingly difficult to find replacement paper, since adding machines were as obsolete as 8-track audio tapes. But it meant a lot to her, even though no one remembered the identity of the gift's donor.

"You go," Mom said. "I really don't feel much like going out today."

"Really? It's sunny out. You need to get out and enjoy it."

"You enjoy it for me," Mom said. "I only need a few things this week. I think I'll stay home and work this puzzle."

I donned my reading glasses and squinted at the list, in light pencil. Mom never used a pen---just pencils. She kept them sharpened with a small plastic, hand-twist sharpener she kept in the tiny drawer in the round table next to her rocking chair. I had stocked her kitchen with dozens of pens, but now whenever I managed to locate one in her house, it was dry.

----

3 or 4 grapefruit, ruby red (only)

1 pint of cherry tomatoes

Seedless red grapes (must be seedless)

Orange juice, no pulp

Bottle of Tums

2 Bottles of Sprite

Dozen eggs (large) (check them for cracks)

Blue Bonnet margarine, in tubs

Frozen blueberries

1 pkg frozen Snickers bars

6 Lean Cuisines (8 if on sale)

Dawn dish soap (I like the green one to go with my kitchen)

1 box Quaker Oat Squares

Keebler peanut butter chocolate chip cookies

Butterfinger minis

M&M peanut, fun size

Pringles, regular, red can

Little Debbies oatmeal pies

Mini donuts

Toilet paper

Brawny paper towels

Puffs in the square box

The list seldom varied. Ever since Mom had learned how to use a microwave, shortly before Dad died, she switched from actual cooking to heating up Lean Cuisine frozen dinners. Breakfast was always a half grapefruit, cereal with blueberries, and coffee. Lunch was half a sandwich, usually peanut butter and jelly, with carrot sticks. Dinner was a Lean Cuisine.

"Are you going to have enough money?" Mom asked. "Get my purse and I'll give you some."

"I pay with a check, remember?"

"Then how do I reimburse you?" she asked.

"No, Mom, I write a check from your account, remember?"

"I'm surprised they take it at the store. They know me, and they know you're not me," Mom said.

I showed her a check, bearing her name and mine at the top.

"Well, I'll be darned," Mom declared. "When did this happen? Did I give you permission to form a joint account? I don't remember doing that."

"It was your idea, remember? You were getting a little confused with your bills, so I took over paying them from your account."

"How long has this been going on?" she asked, frowning.

"Almost three years now," I answered.

"I was wondering how my bills were being paid. So how do you get them?"

"We changed your mailing address to my house."

"I wondered why I wasn't getting any mail. Is it okay with the post office?" she asked.

"Oh, they don't care one way or the other," I told her. Mom thought for a minute, then nodded.

"Well, I guess it's okay. I know I can trust you," she said, patting my hand. "But be sure to bring me the receipt so I can reimburse you."

When I got back to the house, an Indians game was playing full blast on her TV. She was in her chair, her feet up on the ottoman, sound asleep, snoring loudly.

I put away the groceries, threw away the long-dead plants on the kitchen table, put a few pieces in the jigsaw puzzle, turned down the TV volume to something slightly lower than deafening, and tiptoed out.

From that day on, Mom left the house less and less. At first, she would give me some excuse, such as waiting for a phone call from her best friend Mary Lou, who lived in Florida. Other times she didn't want to miss the Indians game. After awhile, she didn't bother with an excuse. She just wanted to stay home.

Years later, Mary Lou confided that Mom had told her why she would not leave the house. She was convinced that Dad would be coming for her soon, and she wanted him to be able to find her, so she stayed home. She didn't want to miss him when he came for her.

Chapter Five

August 28, 2012

"Who's putting D's in my trees?"

By late summer of 2012, Mom was relying on her four-pronged cane all the time. It had taken her more than a year to accept the necessity of relying on a cane. But after a few months, it became a familiar friend, undoubtedly saving her from some nasty falls.

One Thursday afternoon in August, on an overcast, steel-grey day heavy with moisture, I found Mom sitting in the TV room, in her cushioned maple, back torturing rocking chair, her feet up on the ottoman we had given her for Christmas. We called that chair a torture chamber. It was extremely uncomfortable and guaranteed a back ache to anyone other than Mom sitting there. She, however, loved it.

Dad had bought it for her in 1960, so she endured all the aches and pains it caused. The TV was blasting well over the 100 decibels that can cause permanent damage to one's hearing. The reverberations were very painful. Before saying a word, I snapped up the remote control and set it to MUTE.

Whew. My ear drums thanked me.

"Hi, Mom," I yelled, kissing her on the cheek.

"Did I have it up too loud?" Mom asked. "I couldn't tell. Must need a new hearing aid battery. Maybe you can change it for me while you're here."

Mom changed her hearing aid batteries constantly. I could tell, because we were always running to Drug Mart for batteries. Each battery was supposed to last about a week, and there were several in a pack, but I suspected she was changing them every two or three days, or maybe even more than once a day, based on how often she ran through a card of them.

She left the "old" batteries scattered around everywhere. It was impossible to determine whether they were old ones or new ones, functioning or not. I took out her old battery and put in one that I hoped was new.

"I want to show you something," Mom said. "I'm glad you are here. Something strange is going on."

She stood up and motioned me to the window across from her chair. She frowned in concentration, then pointed outside.

I crossed the tiny room and peered out the window.

"What am I supposed to see?"

"Don't you see them? You mean my old eyes are sharper than yours?" she demanded.

"I don't see anything out of the ordinary," I said. "Just the big maple tree out in the yard."

"Don't tell me you can't see them! They're plain as day!" Her voice was shrill.

"What, Mom? What do you see?"

"Don't you see all those D's?" Mom demanded. "I counted 14 of them. Someone has hung D's in the tree, and I don't know why."

Uh oh.

"I don't see them," I told her gently, as I felt the hairs on the back of my neck stand at attention.

"Well, they're there, all right," Mom sniffed indignantly. "I can't believe you can't see them. All those D's hanging on the tree. Why would somebody do that? What do they mean?"

"Are they capital D's or small d's?" I asked her.

"Don't get smart with me!" she said. "They're big D's! And they're everywhere! What could they mean?"

I decided to play along.

"Danger? December? Dad? Diane?" I ventured. "Beats me."

Mom sighed and shook her head.

"I wish I knew," she said. "Go out there and see if there are any footprints around the base of the tree, or a ladder up against it. I can't imagine why anyone would want to do that. I don't ever see anyone do it, so they are probably hanging them at night while I'm asleep."

I just stared at her, dumbfounded, with no words, whether or not they started with D.

"Well, go on," Mom demanded. "Go out there and find out who's doing this. Oh, and while you're out there, could you fill the bird feeder? It's hard for me to manage it, and I don't want to chance running into anybody out there messing with my tree."

As summer gradually gave way to Fall, at each visit, Mom would report how many D's people had hung in the tree on any given day. Each time, it was more, and the people were apparently now hanging them in all the other trees in the yard as well. 14, then 21, then 28, 37, 41, 45.

"I counted 55 of them today," Mom announced one day in early October. "I wonder why so many?"

"Well, maybe you can see more of them because the leaves are changing color," I suggested. "I would imagine all of them will disappear once the leaves are gone." (At least I hope so, I added silently.)

Whoever was decorating Mom's maple trees with D's must have been sensitive to cold, or maybe they had joined the great annual migration from Ohio to Florida, because once the leaves were gone and the branches coated with snow, the D's apparently disappeared, and to my great relief, they didn't return in the spring.

Mom never mentioned them again.

Chapter Six

October 28, 2012

"Halloween is Scary. I'm going to bed."

By late October, Mom started going to bed earlier and earlier. I thought she was just tired, and once the sun set, taking the daylight away, it took her energy with it.

I was only partly right.

When Dad was alive, they had a daily routine that seldom varied, regardless of their location or whether it was Daylight Savings Time. Shortly after sunset, Mom would lock all the doors, turn on the lamp on a table in the front window, and generally make the rounds, like an intrepid night watchman, checking that the house was secure for the night. Once she was satisfied that everything was locked, she would go upstairs to the bedroom, change into her nightgown, robe, and slippers, rejoin Dad downstairs, and settle into her extremely uncomfortable cushioned maple rocker while Dad sat in the equally uncomfortable, but matching, cushioned maple rocking love seat, surrounded by pillows.

They would watch either an Indians baseball game, classic movie, or PBS nature programs from 8 to 11.

On the stroke of 11, Mom would stand up, announce that she was going to bed, and Dad would tell her he would be up after the weather. After the week's forecast, at approximately 11:18, he would turn off the TV, turn off the lamp on the round table, turn on the hall light at the bottom of the stairs, and make his way up.

Their routine never varied. But as the years went on, without Dad, Mom established her own pattern. After her Lean Cuisine dinner at 5:30 on the dot, she would carefully wash the few dishes, including the plastic Lean Cuisine container, let everything drain on a rack, and struggle upstairs to her bedroom, clinging to the railing, one careful step at a time. Once upstairs, she would wash at the bathroom sink, change into her nightgown, turn down her bed covers, and struggle back downstairs to settle into the padded but extremely uncomfortable maple rocker.

If the Indians were on, she would watch the game intently. If not, she would channel surf in search of a game show or soap opera replay. By 8 or sunset, whichever came first, she would turn off the TV, make her rounds locking every door and window, turn off all the downstairs lights, struggle back upstairs one stair at a time, and close all the interior doors upstairs, so no light could be seen from outside.

She would brush her teeth, close her bedroom door, place something heavy in front of the door, and get into bed with a small dish of M&Ms mixed with dry cereal. She would turn on the bedside TV and a small lamp hanging over the bed, work a few crossword puzzles or read, and fall asleep with the TV blasting.

Her bedtime routine differed only one night of the year: Halloween. The holiday terrified her, after the memorable night of October 31, 1963, when a gang of neighbor kids surrounded the house and banged on the windows, drawing on them with soap, or, worse, crayons. They ran around most of the houses in the neighborhood that night, but although the incident lasted for only two or three minutes, it frightened Mom and ruined Halloween for her for the rest of her life.

So every Halloween night, as I filled a big bowl of candy at my house and placed it next to the door in anticipation of hordes of cute little trick-or-treaters, Mom, at her house, would go through her nightly routine mid-afternoon, closing up the house, struggling upstairs by 4 p.m., cowering in her bed waiting in terror for darkness to fall, trying desperately to fall asleep before someone came to attack her or the house.

As time went on, she would begin to panic if she was away from home at 3 p.m., regardless of the calendar. During Christmas, birthdays, and other celebrations at Gary's house, she would demand that someone take her home at about 3 p.m. "I have to be home before dark," was her panicked explanation, but she would divulge no details.

Her annual Halloween ritual gradually became a nightly event, as she would go to bed well ahead of the sun every night. Once I asked her what was scaring her every evening.

"I just don't want anyone driving into my driveway at night," she explained. "I don't want visitors at night."

"Who would visit you at night?" I asked.

"Oh, I don't know. Maybe your cousins from Ashtabula. They'd show up without calling first, and I don't want company coming unannounced."

"Mom, they haven't been to see you in decades, even if they remembered how to get here," I said. "I'm sure if they wanted to visit, they would call you first."

"Well, I don't want anyone coming here at night," she said. End of discussion.

So every afternoon she would barricade herself in her bedroom, in the darkened house, with heavy objects placed against her bedroom door, with every exterior door locked, safe in the fortress of her mind.

Chapter Seven

May 13, 2013

"GOT ANY SAFETY PINS?"

One day I noticed an angry purple bruise on Mom's shoulder.

"Where did you get that?" I asked as I examined it closely and looked, in vain, for others.

"I'm not quite sure," was her response. "It just appeared. Or maybe it might have been Monday, when I fell down the basement stairs."

The basement stairs were steep, dark, and rickety, with a shaky railing that had been repaired at least a dozen times. The scary part was, at the very bottom of the stairs was a concrete block wall. Mom's washer and dryer were down there, as were Dad's workbench and drafting table. The latter two items had been pretty much gathering dust since Dad passed, unless Gary needed to find a part to fix something.

But the washer and dryer were still being used on Mondays, which everyone knew was the traditional Laundry Day in most American homes, or at least in Mom's. Monday was Laundry Day, Tuesday was Ironing Day, Wednesday was Marketing Day, Thursday was Housecleaning Day, and Friday was Baking Day. The schedule was carved in stone and never varied.

Laundry Day began right after breakfast. Mom used the old 1920s era wringer washer that she had inherited from Grandma in 1947. It was galvanized tin, had a square tub with rounded corners, and sat on a short platform, with a small motor underneath. Over the tub loomed the wringer, with its double cylinders on a metal frame that swiveled.

Mom would tell me horror stories about the little girl she once knew who played with the wringer and got her arm stuck in it. She was scarred for life, she said. Years later, I realized it was in all probability a cautionary tale designed to keep curious little girls away from the machine.

Each Laundry Day Mom would fill the washer's tub with a hose connected to two galvanized stationary tubs with hot and cold faucets, and then fill one of the tubs with rinse water. After carefully measuring and adding a level cup of powdered Oxydol to the machine, she would fill it with either whites, lights, or darks, from separate piles on the basement floor.

The load of whites went in first, because they needed the hottest water. As the water in the washing machine gradually cooled, the other loads would go in, with the darks last. By then, the water in the machine was cool, if not actually cold.

If washing the whites, she would add a cup of Chlorox and maybe a little bluing, which would render the clothes blinding white.

She kept a corrugated wooden washboard for scrubbing stains, such as collar rings. She would rub

Fels Naptha soap on the offending spot, then rub it up and down on the washboard. When she was satisfied that the spot had disappeared, the now stain-free garment would join the others in the machine.

Sometimes the most stubborn stains got a dab of Lestoil and another rubbing, this time with a wooden handled laundry brush. No stain was safe from Mom. After all, her reputation among the neighbors was at stake. Mom's reputation among her peers depended on how clean, neat, and wrinkle-free her family's clothing looked.

Mom's washing machine made a rhythmic slosh-slosh-SLOSH; slosh-slosh-SLOSH as the agitator spun back and forth and the Oxydol worked its magic.

Once Mom was convinced that the load was clean, she would run each garment through the wringer, which squeezed the soap and water from the item, which would then go into one of the galvanized stationary tubs, filled with water.

After a good rinse, she would swivel the wringer into position and wring each garment again, sometimes twice, before she was convinced it was no longer dripping wet. On sunny days, she would toss the clean, damp clothes into a basket, which she would haul upstairs and outside to the clothesline in the back yard.

First, she would wipe the line with a worn-out towel that she kept specifically for that purpose. When she was satisfied that the line was clean and free from bird droppings, she would fish two wooden clothespins from a cotton hanging bag suspended on the clothes line. One by one, each wet garment was pinned onto the line. Shirts and dresses were usually pinned upside down, by their hems.

On rainy or snowy days, she would hang the clothes on lines in the basement, where they would drip onto the plain concrete floor. Towels went into the old 1954 era electric dryer, but everything else, including socks and underwear, went onto a line.

Mom insisted the clothes always smelled cleaner when hung outside. This was especially true with sheets.

As Mom and Dad aged, the three of us kids got the bright idea to replace the old wringer washer with a new automatic model. We knew it would probably result in a fight, but doing laundry would be so much easier for Mom with a new washer and dryer. So one winter, while Mom and Dad were in Florida, my brother Ken arranged for the old wringer washer and ancient electric dryer to be removed and replaced with a brand new, basic washer and dryer.

To our surprise, Mom seemed to adapt enthusiastically to this drastic change in her lifestyle. Maybe she realized how much easier it was to keep her clothes clean. Ever since, she had used the new machines with ease until the present day.

Convinced that the bruise wasn't serious, this time, I asked Mom how she fell.

"I can't rightly remember," she said. "But I do know I only fell down a step or two. I must have hit my shoulder on the wall at the bottom of the stairs. Honestly, it doesn't hurt."

"Were you carrying a laundry basket?" I asked.

"I really don't remember; maybe," she said.

When I related the fall and the bruise to Ed and Gary, we decided that Mom shouldn't be using those rickety stairs anymore. Of course, that would mean that SOMEONE would need to take over doing Mom's laundry. At least we wouldn't be worrying about her falling down the stairs.

The following Saturday, Ed and Gary went down into Mom's basement while Mom and I worked one of her favorite zigsaw puzzles at the kitchen table.

"What are the boys doing down there?" she asked, peering suspiciously in the general direction of the basement door.

"Oh, probably checking the dehumidifier or fixing something," I hedged.

A few minutes later, my resourceful husband and brother emerged from the basement. I noticed that Gary was trying to conceal a small metal part behind his hand.

"What's that?" the maternal detective asked, her eyes squinting in suspicion. You could never pull the wool over her eyes. Ask us about the many unsuccessful attempts over the teen years to smuggle contraband past her eagle eye.

"The washer is broken," Gary announced, neglecting to add how it had come about.

"I'll need to replace this part," he lied. Lying to Mom had been a necessity since we were kids, and we had developed it into an art form out of self preservation.

"So now what do I do?" she asked. We were ready for that question.

"Just put all of your dirty clothes into the laundry basket in your room," I said. "Once or twice a week, I'll take it home with me and take care of it for you."

"I hate to ask you to do that," Mom said, trying to conceal her relief at the idea that she wouldn't have to do that chore anymore.

From then on, I took over the laundry duty. I made a sign for the basement door that read: DO NOT GO DOWNSTAIRS. STEPS ARE BROKEN. Mom was always very good at obeying signs.

When I brought home the basket to wash the clothes, I noticed something odd.

Her pull-on slacks had dozens of large safety pins, including ancient plastic-capped diaper pins, on the insides of the waist bands.

Hmmm.

Over the past couple of years, Mom had gradually lost a great deal of weight, despite her continued

73

fondness for M&Ms and Little Debbies. A wave of guilt washed over me, as I realized that she had gone from a hefty size 18 to about a size 6 in the space of roughly five years. The change had been so gradual that although I saw her two to three times per week, I really hadn't noticed that her clothes no longer fit.

So I found her favorite clothing brands online and ordered a dozen color-coordinated outfits, smaller underwear, five or six high-necked nylon nightgowns, three housecoats, several sweaters and sweatshirts, a few floral short sleeved pullover tops, and a couple of jackets.

Then I noticed that her shoes were completely worn out. How could I have let that happen?

Back to the online stores, to select three or four pairs of slip-on canvas shoes and two pairs of slippers. When all of the new items arrived, Mom declared it was Christmas and happily tried everything on.

Three weeks later, when I walked into the house, I noticed that Mom was wearing her all-time favorite raspberry colored pants, held up with safety pins all around. The laundry basket contained only her old clothes and none of the new ones.

"I'm used to these," was her explanation. "Besides, Dad picked out most of these for me, and I like the colors better. I'll save the fancy new clothes for dressing up on special occasions."

Ed, who somehow actually gets enjoyment from purging possessions, came up with a great solution. The following Sunday, he backed our oversized GMC

Acadia up to Mom's front door and carried in a roll of huge trash bags.

While I distracted Mom downstairs at the back of the house, Ed took the trash bags upstairs to Mom's room, opened her closets, and filled the bags with anything bigger than a size 10. He stuffed the back of our car with the clothes, which we would donate to charity.

"Who's upstairs?" Mom asked as her selective hearing kicked in.

"It's just Ed; he's fixing the toilet," I lied innocently.

But Ed was just getting started. Over the next six or seven Sundays, he filled our car with old rugs, worn out towels, dead plants, the old broken vacuum cleaner, and anything else he thought should be pitched. I managed to rescue a few treasures from the piles---one pile to donate and one to throw away—but he did a great job of de-cluttering the house, which also made it safer for Mom to navigate.

Then he focused on the basement, which had boxes and boxes of Mom's lifetime collection of Mrs. Butterworth's bottles, which she was somehow convinced would be valuable in the future.

"These will pay for my grandchildren's college educations someday," she would brag confidently. We didn't have the heart to disagree with her.

So, over the next few Sundays, our Acadia got filled with eight boxes of Mrs. Butterworth bottles, six boxes of miscellaneous canned goods dating to the mid 1950s that Dad had placed there when he declared that the basement would be the family's Designated Bomb Shelter, four boxes of various dried-out cleaning products, two more bags of old clothes, and several small appliances---all of them broken, that Dad had set aside to fix "some day."

For the first time in 50-plus years, the shelves under the stairs, all handcrafted by Dad in 1947, were empty.

Next came the kitchen, which I tackled after much procrastination. I waited till Mom was napping deeply one afternoon. I opened several trash bags and opened one of the cupboards, as dozens of foam egg cartons tumbled out and hit me on the head. Good thing they were foam.

There must have been 30 or 40 of them, all in pastel Easter colors.

The next cabinet was neatly stacked with black plastic containers from Lean Cuisine entrees, all carefully washed out by hand, complete with lids. They all joined the egg cartons in the now-bulging trash bag.

One by one, the cabinets yielded stacks and stacks of plastic bowls, empty foam containers from Heinens' produce department, empty cardboard cereal boxes, empty paper towel cores and toilet paper rolls, and empty margarine tubs, all cleaned and neatly stacked.

One drawer was stuffed with used aluminum foil. Another was full of old sponges and disposable washrags.

I dragged four huge, bulging trash bags outside and heaved them into the back of the Acadia. Then I remembered one more cabinet, above the stove, where Mom kept spices and cooking condiments.

She hadn't been in that cabinet in probably 10 years, because she could no longer reach it. I got a step ladder and dug in. There were hundreds of dusty little bottles looking back at me in alarm. At least I imagined they knew at some level that their day of reckoning had arrived.

I filled a smaller but stronger trash bag with little metal cans or glass or plastic bottles of dry mustard, garlic powder, minced garlic, garlic salt, (dozens of each), cumin, coriander, sage, oregano, basil, dill, dried orange peel, salt substitute, carroway seeds, poppy seeds, sesame seeds, nutmeg, ginger, curry powder, bay leaf, cardamom, cloves---both whole and powdered, fennel, paprika, rosemary, turmeric, thyme, gravy mix—both chicken and beef, bouillon cubes (ditto), parsley, and tarragon.

Most of the bottles were coated with cooking grease over decades. There were at least four jars of each spice.

There were larger bottles of Worcestershire sauce, liquid smoke, Wesson oil, popcorn oil, and apple cider vinegar.

There was one recently purchased jar of cinnamon, and a shaker container of cinnamon and sugar. I reasoned that they must be fairly new, because Mom loved cinnamon and sugar on toast.

I moved the cinnamon containers to her coffee cabinet, filled and removed the trash bags, and scrubbed out the now-empty cabinet.

"What are you doing?" asked Eagle Eye, in the same tone she used when I spent too much time in my boyfriend's car in the driveway at the end of a date.

"Oh, just cleaning out a cabinet," I replied, mustering as much innocence as I could.

"Well, it probably needed it," Mom admitted. "I haven't been able to find anything in there in years."

No kidding.

Mom got up and inspected the cabinets one by one, each now relatively clutter-free.

"Where did everything go?" she demanded. "I was saving all those containers for the grandkids. They may be able to use them in their houses. You never know when you'll need a plastic container for something."

"Mom, the containers from the store are only supposed to be used one time, then thrown away," I told her. "It's a health law or something. They can only be used once."

"Now that's ridiculous," she snorted. "I washed everything thoroughly in hot water. There's nothing wrong with these containers. Somebody can find some use for them. When I was young, during the Great Depression, we reused everything. Now they call it recycling. Or they just throw away perfectly good things with a lot of use still in them. I will find a use for them someday. Put everything back where you found it."

So, after 60-plus years of practice out of necessity, I lied to my mother, fingers crossed behind my back. I assured her that I knew of several teachers who could use them for art projects and crafts. Picturing happy little children making egg carton bunnies or growing plants from seeds in the plastic cartons, Mom graciously granted me permission to remove them all.

"They were starting to crowd my cabinets, anyway," she said.

By October, I had to do it all again. All, that is, except the spice cabinet. Mom couldn't reach up there anymore.

Chapter Eight

"Where's Mom?"

February 27, 2014

As I carried four bags of the week's provisions into the kitchen and set them down on the counter, Mom was in the adjoining TV room, in her favorite torture device of a chair, her feet propped up on the ottoman, television full blast. She was munching from a bag of peanut M&Ms, her eyes glued to Days of Our Lives.

"How are you doing, Mom?" I asked as I grabbed the remote and hit the MUTE button, saving my ear drums. I kissed her on the cheek.

"Do you know that these people on TV go to bed with just anybody?" she marveled. "I mean, they barely know each other, but they go out to dinner, and the next thing you know, they are in bed. Stupid women. It's like they figure they need to reward the man just for taking them out to dinner. No wonder the world is in such a mess."

"If it upsets you, don't watch," I said. "Find a nice travel show, or something on the History Channel."

"I forget what numbers they are," she groused. "I liked the good old days when we had three choices: channel three, channel five, and channel eight. Much easier with fewer decisions."

"I made you a cheat sheet with your favorite channels listed," I said, glancing around the room for the neon pink card that listed her preferred channels. Last year, Gary's daughter Nicole got the brilliant idea to use electrical tape to block off confusing or otherwise unwanted functions on Mom's TV remote. She didn't need to go into various video sources, and an on-demand search or DVR command was way beyond her capabilities. The only visible buttons were the on/off, channel changer, and volume.

I found the cheat sheet in her end table drawer and helped her find a program on the animals of Australia. She cranked up the volume all the way back to PAINFUL and sat back, contented for the next few minutes. She sipped her favorite Sprite from an ancient, tall iced tea glass, patterned in fleurs de lis, that once held damson plum preserves at the old A&P. The drinking glass came free when you bought the Large Economy Size. In the summer of 1958.

I put away her groceries and made her lunch: half of a peanut butter and jelly sandwich, a small sweet gherkin, a handful of Pringles chips (the regular flavor, from the red can), and a Little Debbie oatmeal cream pie, her favorite.

"Do I owe you any money?" she asked.

"No, Mom. I paid for it with your credit card."

"And they took it? They must know that you're not me," she said, horrified.

"It's a joint account," I answered yet again, for probably the 46th time. "Then I pay all the bills from our joint checking account. Remember?"

"When did that happen?" she asked, accusation creeping into her voice.

"About ten years ago," I said in the soothing voice I had been working hard to develop over the past several years.

"Why didn't anyone ask my permission?"

"It actually was your idea, Mom," I soothed. "Remember? You were getting all kinds of junk mail, and managing your checkbook was starting to get confusing. So you turned over your bill paying to me."

"I was wondering why I haven't seen any bills in the last few days," she replied, nodding. She settled back in her chair and popped four M&M's into her mouth.

"You didn't eat very much," I observed.

"I wasn't real hungry. I had a big breakfast. By the way, I used up my last grapefruit."

"I know," I answered. "I just brought you six more. That should last you most of the week."

"Are they ruby reds?" she asked. "That's the only kind I like. The plain ones are too sour."

"Yes. I know."

She settled further into her chair and started humming an old hymn, "Blessed Assurance, Jesus is Mine."

I remembered that one from a long time ago. As a child, I had loved sitting next to Mom's mother, Grandma Jessie, in church every Sunday, dressed in my carnation pink Sunday dress complete with layers of tulle petticoats, black patent leather Red Goose shoes, white ruffled socks, and white hat and gloves. Grandma's sweet soprano voice would joyfully belt out the beloved old tunes, creating lifelong favorites for me.

When I was 12, Grandma Jessie was diagnosed with "hardening of the arteries," which was another way of describing dementia. The term "Alzheimer's disease" was unknown, at least to us, in 1960. We just knew that Grandma was becoming so forgetful that she would wander the house at night, sometimes walking outside during the daytime and getting lost, and gradually she would forget who we were, and basics like how to use the bathroom.

Mostly out of fear of her getting hurt, or starting a fire, or running out into the street in her nightgown, Mom had to arrange for Grandma to move to one of the few nursing homes in the area, where Grandma was cared for and watched closely. Mom visited her almost every day, burdened with guilt at putting her beloved "Mom" away and paying strangers to care for her. In the old days, if the Grandma beat the odds and lived a long life, she spent her declining days being lovingly cared for by succeeding generations.

These days, with the old folks living longer, caring for them was overwhelming, especially when their behavior was unpredictable and possibly dangerous to themselves and to the rest of the family.

Grandma finally succumbed to the disease on April 24, 1962, in a nursing home four miles from our house. I was 14, and devastated to lose the sweet, loving lady I had adored my whole life.

More than a half century has gone by since then, but I still miss her. We all do.

Twenty years later, Mom's oldest brother, my Uncle Russell, was diagnosed with what was by then identified as Alzheimer's Disease, with virtually identical symptoms to what Grandma had had. Over a little more than a year, he became increasingly baby-like. It was very painful to witness, and even more painful to learn that this degenerative disease of the brain tends to be genetic.

Thoughts such as these ran through my head frequently during the next several years, as more and more, Mom increasingly demonstrated similar symptoms.

Over the next several months, she began humming constantly. At first, they were actual, recognizable tunes. "You Are My Sunshine," "The Old Rugged Cross," "Rudolph, the Red Nosed Reindeer," "Stranger in Paradise," "Tumblin' Tumbleweed," and the Mr. Clean jingle. Whatever popped into her head.

As time went on, the recognizable melodies degenerated into tunes only Mom knew, then gradually into just a constant hmmmmm, hmmmmm, HMMMMM, hmmm, hmmmmm, HMMMM, every waking moment except when she was eating. I don't think she was in the least aware that she was doing it. A nurse friend suggested that maybe Mom was convincing herself that she could still hear. I guess that was as good a theory as any other.

Late one afternoon, as I pondered what to make for dinner at my house, the landline phone rang, with the caller ID displaying Mom's number.

"Hi, Mom. What's up?" I asked, figuring that something probably was. Sure enough, heavy breathing and humming at the other end.

"Where's Mom?" Mom asked, in her most worried tone.

Oh, dear.

"I mean, is she in a nursing home somewhere?" Mom asked. "I know I haven't talked to her in quite some time, and she's probably wondering what happened to me. I must have lost her number because I can't find it. Do you have it? I'd like to give her a call."

I thought briefly of how to tell her without upsetting her. I opted for the truth.

"Mom," I said gently. "Grandma has been gone for more than 50 years. She died in 1962."

"She did? Where was I?" she asked, clearly agitated.

"You were there," I said in as even a tone as I could manage. "You planned the funeral."

"Well, what happened? Was she in an accident or something?"

Hedging, I answered, "She was very old. Think about it. She was born in 1881. If she were still living today, how old would she be?"

"I don't know. Probably pretty old," she said.

"If Grandma were still living today, she would be 133," I said.

"That's pretty old," Mom conceded. "I was wondering about her, and why I hadn't heard from her in the last few days. I thought something had happened to her."

We had the exact same conversation, virtually word for word, every day for the next several weeks. Finally, out of desperation, I printed a sticker: "Jessie Licklider: BORN SEPT 19, 1881. DIED APRIL 24, 1962." I stuck it onto the glass at the bottom of the framed photo of Grandma, circa 1952, that Mom always kept next to her chair.

It worked, most of the time.

Mom would say, "I have a really nice picture of Mom here next to me. Did you know she died in 1962? So long ago. I still miss her every day, and wish she was here to take care of me."

One night in June, she called to ask me again for Grandma's number. After explaining it one more time, I made a point of checking the photo next to

Mom's chair on my next visit to her house. Sure enough. The sticker had fallen off.

I replaced that sticker four times.

Chapter Nine

"There's a Strange Woman in My House."

September 18, 2014

As summer started to wane, it became clear that Mom needed more help than I could give her with my three visits each week.

Mom always loved dogs, and often dog-sat for us over the years, and was especially fond of our first dog, Sandy, who considered Mom and Dad's house her vacation home. They took her home with them frequently, and it was our Sandy who reacted and alerted them when their house was broken into all those years ago.

Over the decades, and for years after Dad passed away, our dogs loved going to Mom's for a visit, because she always had treats. Our daughter Megan's rescue mixed breed, Kobey, was no exception.

Kobey stayed with us from time to time, sometimes for stretches of several weeks. He was a happy dog, eager to please, but he had an adventurous side too. If he ever got loose, he would consider his temporary freedom a vacation, which sometimes lasted several frantic hours as we scattered to round him up. I think he considered his occasional escapes a fun way to get everyone's attention.

Mom always loved Kobey's visits, and the feeling was mutual. She loved petting him and having long discussions with him, and he returned the favor by sitting next to her, his neck conveniently positioned for frequent rubbing.

During one of our visits, I brought along a check for her to sign, so that I could deposit it into her account. After she signed it, I told her I would take it to the bank, and called Kobey's name to go with me.

"Oh, let him stay," Mom said. "You'll only be gone a few minutes, and he's such good company. I'll watch him and he'll be fine."

I hesitated. Mom had watched all of our dogs for years, but in her current level of confusion, I didn't know whether I could trust her not to let him out. Her yard was not fenced, and she was too frail to take him on a leash.

"We'll be fine," Mom reiterated. "Just go."

"Well, okay," I relented. "He's been out to go to the bathroom, so he won't need to go out. Just keep him in the house with you. I'll be back in 20 minutes."

Kobey wagged his tale in apparent approval, an innocent expression on his furry face.

"Just promise me that you'll keep him in the house the whole time," I said. "If he gets out, he'll take off and we'll never get him back. He doesn't know this neighborhood, and his license tag is from his home county."

Kobey wagged again, apparently promising to be good.

"Don't worry about a thing. We'll be fine," Mom assured me, patting Kobey's head.

"Promise me you won't let him out under any circumstances," I said.

"Of course; I promise," she said. "Now go."

The bank was two miles away, a five minute trip. As I pulled up to the drive-through, my cell rang. The ID said Mom.

"The dog got out," she announced.

"What?!!! How did that happen? You promised not to let him out five minutes ago!"

"I did? Well, he went to the door and I thought he needed to go to the bathroom, so I opened the door, but instead of finding his spot, he just disappeared. I called 'Sandy' several times, but he didn't come back. Should I go after him?"

"No! Just stay there! I'll be back in five minutes! Don't go anywhere!"

"I won't," Mom promised.

Not waiting to explain to the smiling teller on the screen that I didn't have time for a transaction, I drove off, praying that Kobey stayed near the house, but knowing full well he was probably heading for the busy main street a block away. Megan, and especially the granddaughters, would be devastated if anything happened to Kobey.

Back in Mom's driveway, I dashed into the house for Kobey's leash.

"Well, for cryin' out loud," Mom said when she spotted me. "What are you doing here?"

"I need Kobey's leash," I said, trying not to show my rising panic.

"Oh? Did you bring Kobey with you? Where is he?" Mom asked.

"That is the question," I told her. "I have to go find him. I'll be back."

In the front yard I began calling his name, wondering which direction I should take. Not wanting to waste any precious time, I decided to head in the direction of the main street, the most dangerous, and most likely, path he took.

"You lookin' for a dog?" called one woman from the front porch of the house where the Claytons once lived.

"Yes! Have you seen him?"

"Yellow lab?" she asked.

Close enough.

"Yes. Somehow he got out," I answered, beginning to puff from the exertion.

"I saw him heading toward the church parking lot. Hope you catch him before he gets to the road."

"Thanks! So do I!"

I ran as fast as my aging, arthritic legs would go, praying I wasn't too late. As I reached the Methodist Church parking lot, I spotted a wagging yellow tail in between some boxwood bushes. Relieved, I held out a treat I had grabbed on my way out from Mom's, and forced my voice to be calm.

"Kobey! What a good boy you are! Would you like a treat?"

His wag got faster. Lucky for me, the dog couldn't resist a treat. Soon he was on the leash and happily padding alongside me.

"Well, hello, Sandy," Mom said when we got back into the house. "I'm glad you came for a visit."

Kobey wagged in response. If she wanted to call him Sandy, it was okay with him, as long as the end result was a treat.

"Mom, I wasn't able to deposit your check," I said. "I'll have to do it another time."

"Why don't you just go now?" she asked. "I'll be glad to watch Sandy."

"Uh, no thanks. I don't have time."

We never tried that again.

As time went on, I noticed that Mom, always meticulous to the point of vanity, stopped combing her hair or applying makeup, began wearing the same outfit every day, and it was increasingly stained with grease spots. When I questioned her about it, she would insist that she had just put this outfit on fresh that morning.

It seemed to distress her that I would help her change into clean clothes whenever I arrived.

"Why do I need to change?" she would whine. "This is clean. I just washed and ironed it myself yesterday."

She had stopped taking baths because it was too risky and difficult to get in and out of the tub. She didn't have a shower in her house, so she would just wash at the sink every morning. To my relief, that had become ingrained in her to the point that it was automatic. She was conscientious about it, which made our lives much easier.

But every day was a struggle to get her to put on fresh underwear and clothes. She would argue that what she had on was perfectly clean. The only person who could convince her to change her clothes was Nicole, Gary's daughter and Mom's granddaughter.

Nicole, a strawberry blonde in her mid twenties, may have reminded Mom of herself in her younger days. That was as good an explanation as any. Mom would fold her arms, stick out her chin, and absolutely refuse to do something if I asked, or even begged her, and ditto with Gary, but for some reason Nicole could just instruct Mom to do something, and Mom would do it.

So we---that is, Gary, his wife Pattie, their daughter Nicole, Ed, and I---decided that it was time to meet and discuss the best strategies for taking care of Mom.

"I can come whenever you need me," Nicole volunteered.

"You live a half hour away, and have your own life, what with your job, and school," I told her. "I really appreciate your wanting to help, but I really think it's time we call in professionals to help. Maybe hire a home health care service."

Because Mom and Dad had led a very frugal life, and Ed had been able to find some excellent investments with their money over the years, there was more than enough in the joint bank account to hire someone to come into the house and make sure Mom was fed, clean, safe, and comfortable.

"Well, it's their money; that's what it's there for," Gary said. "And that way she can stay in the house, like we promised Dad before he died."

After researching several companies, I decided to try Home Safe, a local home healthcare company that a friend had recommended. I set up an appointment for their head nurse and administrator to meet with Mom and do an assessment.

That was easier said than done.

Tuesday morning, two middle-aged ladies from Home Safe met me at Mom's house, shortly after Mom had finished her breakfast and was in her torture chamber chair in the tiny and cramped TV room. I had been unable to convince her to take a seat in the much more accommodating living room.

"Why? What's going on?" Mrs. Suspicious demanded.

"A couple of friends of mine are stopping over to say hello," I lied. "They'd like to see you."

"Why do they want to see me?" Mom asked, the panic starting to show in her voice. Stranger danger, Tom Robinson. Alert. Alert.

"Oh, you'll like them. They're very nice. I went to school with them at Cleveland State. They're in town for today and said they'd like to meet you." Lame, I know. But it was the best I could come up with.

"Seems a little fishy to me," she humphed, but, to my relief, she sat back in her chair, humming, and didn't protest further.

The older woman, with an air of authority, identified herself as Peggy Martin, client director of Home Safe, and introduced me to a stiff-backed, eager looking young lady, Allison Jenkins, a social worker. She looked to me like a high school senior, but I gave her the benefit of the doubt.

I met them on the back porch, told them about the ruse, and asked them not to look official when they talked to Mom.

95

"She's very suspicious by nature, and generally frightened by strangers," I told them. They nodded, said they understood perfectly, and kept their notebooks and briefcases on the porch until the initial ice was broken.

"Mom, this is my friend Peggy from Cleveland State, and her daughter, Allison," I lied. "They're only going to be in the area for a little while, and wanted to see me, so I thought you wouldn't mind if they saw me here."

"No, I don't mind," Mom replied warily, as Peggy and Allison perched on the small rocking love seat near Mom and I took the only other seat in the room, on the steps going upstairs.

"It's so nice to meet you, Mrs. Cuffman," Peggy said. "Diane has told me so much about you. I hear you grew up in Willoughby. That's where I live."

Mom brightened just a bit.

"Yes, I lived on Second Street," Mom told her. "Maybe you know my parents, the Lickliders?"

"No, I'm sorry, I don't," said Peggy, not missing a beat. She began to ask Mom questions about growing up in Willoughby, and Mom began to relax.

After 20 minutes, Allison quietly turned on a small voice recorder. Mom didn't notice as she rattled on about playing basketball in the merchants' league back in the late 1930s. Peggy gradually asked questions about Mom's current life at home.

"Do you do your own laundry?" Peggy asked Mom.

"Every Monday," Mom said proudly.

"Do you cook for yourself?"

"Not as much as I used to, but I get by. I'm not as good a cook as my mom is, though," she admitted.

"When was the last time you saw your doctor?"

Mom thought hard about that one.

"I honestly can't remember," she said. "I think he retired years ago, and I didn't want to break in another one. I don't like going to the doctor, so I only go if it's something serious."

"What medications do you take?"

"Just Tums," Mom said proudly. "I get a little heartburn now and then."

Mom popped Tums like they were candy. Otherwise, she hadn't taken any prescriptions for several years.

Peggy was amazed.

"No prescriptions?" she asked, incredulous.

Mom shook her head emphatically.

"I used to take something for blood pressure, but that was years ago," she told Peggy. "I'm really pretty healthy for an old lady. That's because I never drank or smoked. Thanks for asking."

The interview lasted more than an hour. By then, Mom considered Peggy and Allison old friends.

"What nice ladies!" she exclaimed after they left. "We should have them over more often. I should have offered them some iced tea or Sprite, and some Little Debbies or something. At least put out a bowl of M&Ms. Everybody likes those."

"Maybe for their next visit," I offered.

The following day, Peggy called me with the assessment's results. Naturally, they found a need for a caregiver to come to the house every day for four hours. Mom would have the same person every day, and the assistant would help Mom with bathing and dressing, meal prep, climbing the stairs to her room, and socialization.

"Convincing Mom that she needs this will not be easy," I told her. "Mom is a very stubborn person."

"Don't worry; we can handle it," Peggy said. "I have just the right caregiver in mind. Darlene. She's a sweetheart, and your mother will love her."

We made arrangements for more in-depth physical needs and home safety assessments, and for Darlene to meet Mom and start the following Monday after I signed all the necessary papers. Not to mention, cut them a sizeable check.

"Peggy and Allison are coming for another visit tomorrow," I informed Mom.

"Who?" she asked, narrowing her eyes into a suspicious squint.

"You remember. They came for a visit three days ago. My friend from college."

"Was I here?"

"Yes. You liked them very much."

"Well, they're your friends. You can entertain them if you like, in the living room."

This time, Peggy brought Helen, a nurse practitioner, and Sandra, apparently an expert in elder safety. Mom was reluctant to see them at first, but gradually warmed up to them and answered their questions.

Sandra told me that she was glad to see we had taken so many precautions to remove scatter rugs and to de-clutter the house. She made a few recommendations, including unplugging the stove. Darlene would use the microwave to prepare Mom's meals.

Monday morning I got to Mom's early to set the stage for Darlene's arrival. This was not going to be easy.

"I don't need any help, especially from a stranger," Mom protested, her arms folded defiantly across her once ample, but now flat, chest. "I'm perfectly capable of taking care of myself in my own house, thankyouverymuch."

"Mom, of course you can; Darlene is here to help me," I told her, yet again lying through my teeth to my mother. "She is studying to be a caregiver, and part of her studies involve her volunteering to help an older person take care of their parent. I told her I'd help her out that way. It's not costing anything, and I could use the help."

"You're not getting any younger," Mom conceded. She sighed and thought for a moment. Then she nodded.

"Well, okay, if you say so," Mom said. "If it'll help you. I certainly don't need any help."

That was a huge concession, coming from her.

Darlene was a plump, pleasant lady in her mid forties. She and Mom took to each other immediately. After two hours, they were happily putting together a jigsaw puzzle at the kitchen table.

"You can go home now, if you want," Darlene told me. "We're doing fine. I have your cell number if I have any questions. Relax. I can handle everything."

Over the next few weeks, Mom and Darlene became good friends, and Mom seemed to enjoy having some companionship. I began to spend a little less time at Mom's and a little more time taking care of my own house. I didn't mind writing checks to Home Safe. Mom seemed well cared for and contented.

One Friday morning in late November, we decided to go all-out for Mom's 95th birthday. Darlene found a retired beautician who came to the house and washed and set Mom's baby-fine, wispy hair. I rolled out Mom's old Helene Curtis salon hairdryer, from 1944, that Mom had used in her beauty shop, and I had sat under for countless Toni Home Permanents way back when. It still worked perfectly. Things were built to last in Mom's time.

Mom's face beamed the whole morning, as Clara, the retired beautician, fussed over her, using all of her expertise, bordering on magic, to turn Mom's little wisps of hair into curls. She especially enjoyed Clara asking for her opinion.

The end result was very pretty, and Mom's face glowed in approval. She looked like a teenager preparing for the Junior Prom. Darlene told her she looked like a movie star.

"Well, people always said I looked like Katherine Hepburn, but I always wanted to be more like Betty Grable," Mom admitted.

I bought a purple, sequined pants suit for her, and helped her with her make-up on Saturday, when the family gathered for the big celebration. Darlene had taken the day off to visit her uncle in Toledo.

Gary's wife, Pattie, brought a bucket of fried chicken, Mom's favorite meal, with all the fixings. I brought a cake. All the grandkids and great-grandkids, dressed in their party clothes, brought balloons and hand-lettered signs. Mom seemed overwhelmed, but very pleased to see everyone.

We set up the kitchen table and a card table, and the entire family feasted on Kentucky Fried Chicken, a la Colonel Sanders, in Grandma's kitchen one more time. Gary complimented Mom on the chicken, which had always been her specialty, and her mom's before her.

"Thanks," Mom said, blushing deep pink. "Mom helped me make it this morning. Everybody loves Mom's fried chicken. Relatives we didn't know we had used to come out from St. Louis on Sundays for dinner, unannounced. Mom would never turn anybody away."

After dinner came the cake, with a large "9" candle next to a large "5."

"How old are you, Lois?" Ed asked, knowing the number, as we all did.

"Well, I must be gettin' close to 100," Mom replied. "Some days I feel 110."

Everyone sang Happy Birthday, with the little ones belting it out louder than anyone.

"Which one of you has the birthday?" Mom asked. "Is one of you 9 and another one 5? That's what the cake says."

"No, Mom; It's your birthday. You're 95," I explained.

"Nah. Couldn't be. Me?" she asked, dumbfounded. We encouraged her to make a wish and blow out the candles, which she did in one big puff. The little ones stood next to her, in case she needed help. They loved to blow out candles.

Mom read every word of each birthday card, and marveled at the home-made ones proudly presented by the great-grandkids.

"Which one is Bridget?" she asked. My oldest granddaughter, six, raised her hand. God bless her,

102

she understood Great-Grandma's confusion. She had no problem re-introducing herself to Mom over and over again.

Mom marveled at each gift: a pink flowered robe, two new nightgowns, slippers, perfumed body wash, bags of M&M's, and boxes of Little Debbies.

"I'm all set," she declared. "Now I'm ready for bed."

"You haven't opened all your gifts yet," I told her, and motioned to Bridget, who came forward with a strangely shaped, even more strangely wrapped, gift sporting a big, sloppy bow.

"Happy Birthday, Great Mama," she said to Mom. "This is from all of us kids."

"Thanks, Sweetie," Mom said, beaming. "Did you make this?"

Bridget shook her head. "We just wrapped it."

"Well, you did a nice job," Mom said, patting the top of Bridget's head.

She ripped open the odd-shaped package, to find a stuffed duck, wearing a big straw hat circled with daisies, and sporting a big pink bow.

"He's cute," Mom declared. "He looks like an Oscar. I think I'll call him Oscar."

Bridget started to protest the bird's obvious gender, but I signaled her not to say anything. I made a mental note to explain it to her later, when we were on our way home.

103

I found the little button on "Oscar's" orange webbed foot and pressed it. "He" immediately began swaying from side to side, singing "You Are My Sunshine." Mom clapped her hands with glee and started singing along. She crooked her finger at the little ones and waved it from side to side, as they sang along.

Mom pressed the button to make "him" sing four or five more times, then passed it along to the great-grandchildren, who took turns playing him. Eventually, I confiscated it and put it out of everyone's reach, including Mom's.

"That was my Mom's favorite song," Mom told the kids. "Your great-great grandmother. That's how old the song is."

"Let's hear it again!" little Clare demanded.

"No, that's enough for now. Maybe later," I said, thereby preserving our sanity, what was left of it, anyway.

"One more to open," I told Mom, handing her my gift, a blanket covered in photos of her 95 years of life. One as a baby with her siblings back on the farm in Missouri, one of her with her parents, posed in front of the family's Model T, her high school graduation in 1937, in front of her Lois Beauty Shoppe sign when she opened her salon, her wedding to Dad, and family photos with kids, grandkids, and great-grandkids.

"This is really nice. Wait a minute!" she exclaimed, dumbfounded, as she unfolded the blanket. "There's my house! How did my house get on here?"

104

Photo by photo, she quickly identified the early pictures from long ago, including the big family photo from 1924 that she treasured.

"There I am with my brothers Russell, Buell and Marty, and my sisters Ama and Opal," she marveled. "And Mom and Pop. Where are they now? Weren't they able to come today?"

"No, they weren't able to come," I said softly.

"I can't believe you made me a blanket of my whole life story," Mom said. "And when I'm gone, you can have it. I'll say so in my will." She nodded and patted my hand.

Mom suddenly proclaimed again that she was tired and wanted to go to bed. She said goodnight to everyone, hugged each of the little ones, and let me help her upstairs, get into her nightclothes, go to the bathroom, wash her face, brush her teeth, and get into bed.

"This was a great day, but I'm really tired for some reason," Mom said. "Thanks for putting this together. But tomorrow I want you to give me Mom's phone number so I can find out why she wasn't here. It's too late to call her tonight."

Darlene called me a week before Christmas.

"I'm really sorry, but my sister in Chicago broke her leg and needs me to go help take care of our Mom," Darlene said. "I have to leave right away. I hate to leave you high and dry like this, but the agency will find someone else."

And so the disaster began.

At first, Home Safe sent Marie, a young lady of about 25, who took to Mom immediately. I think Mom thought Marie was one of her granddaughters, because she called her Nicole. Marie didn't mind, and the two of them seemed to get along so well that Ed and I made plans for a much-needed two week vacation in Florida in late January.

"You really need to get away for a little while," my wise husband told me. "You've been taking great care of your mom, but you're burning out. You need a little break. We both do. "

Key Largo is our go-to place for battery recharging. Our friend Ron owns a four acre piece of paradise on the quiet bay side of the island. It was wonderful to sit in the hammock on the dock, my nose in a silly romance novel, not a care in the world.

Just as the handsome but brooding laird of the castle, shirtless and kilted, was about to burst into the damsel's chamber in the tower and rescue her from a forced marriage with the evil duke, my phone rang. Caller ID showed Mom's number.

"COME RIGHT AWAY," Mom whispered. "There's a strange woman in my house. I am going to call the police, but thought I should call you first."

"What does she look like?" I asked, already guessing the answer.

"She's big, young, about 50, and says her name is LaTasha," Mom said. "I don't know why she's here or what she wants. I threw my cane at her. I'm afraid she's gonna rob me. I hid my purse."

"Please let me talk to her," I told Mom.

LaTasha, audibly shaken, said that Marie had come down with the flu, and Home Safe had asked her to fill in at the last minute.

"I've never had a client turn on me like that," LaTasha said.

I apologized to her, told her to go on home, and I would pay her full day's wages. I called Home Safe, and got a recording that their office was closed for the weekend. They left an emergency number for their answering service.

Was this an emergency? Not in the true sense of the word. I hung up without leaving a message, and dialed Gary's cell number.

"Pattie and I are in Pittsburgh, visiting her mother," Gary informed me. Rats.

"Hey, Sis, don't worry. I'll find Nicole and send her over to Mom's," my brother said. "Go back to your vacation. We'll take care of it."

Two hours later, Nicole called to tell me that she had put Grandma to bed.

"She was a little rattled, but she couldn't remember why," Nicole said. "She was humming her distress signal. So I told her a few jokes, and convinced her that she would feel much better after a nap. She's all bundled up in bed and snoring away. I'll stay with her as long as you need me to."

Thank goodness for Nicole.

Monday morning I called Home Safe, apologized for Mom's treatment of LaTasha, and told them if they couldn't send the same care giver every day, we would find other arrangements. They seemed relieved somehow to lose us as a client. The feeling was mutual, but now I was faced with finding another caregiver, one that Mom would accept.

That's when Nicole informed me that she had been let go from her job, and would gladly stay with Grandma till we got back to Ohio.

Crisis averted. Or so I thought.

Chapter Ten

"I'll just turn down the heat."

February 10, 2015

The minute we got back from Florida, I called for another summit meeting with Gary, Pattie, and Ed to decide our next step.

"Would you have any objections to my hiring Nicole to take care of Mom?" I asked my brother, who also happened to be Nicole's dad.

"Would you want her to stay with Mom 24/7?" Gary asked. "I don't think that would work, because Nicole needs to finish her degree, and she needs to be able to come and go on a flexible schedule. I don't think she'd like to be tied down with all that responsibility, but you can ask her. I have no objection."

"Nicole is the only one of us who can get Mom to do anything she doesn't want to do," I said. "Mom listens to her, when anything I tell her is only a mild suggestion. At best, she pretends not to hear."

"It's obvious that Lois needs supervision, at least during the day," Ed said. "And she goes to bed earlier all the time. Maybe Nicole can take care of her during the day, tuck her into bed, and then go to night classes. She wouldn't have to stay there all the time, at least at this stage."

"Mom can still function fairly well, with supervision," I said. "She has her routines, and she stays in the house. Nicole can make sure Mom is washed, dressed, and fed in the morning, maybe do her hair, do a puzzle with her, get her lunch, help her find something on TV, get her dinner, and put her to bed by 7. I can continue to do the marketing, bills, and laundry.

"And because Nicole's her granddaughter, Mom will be comfortable accepting the help," I offered.

Nicole jumped at the chance. A paying job, taking care of Grandma. Win—win—win all around.

Because of her studies and yes, her social life, the schedule would need to be flexible. In turn, Nicole would make sure Mom had enough easy access to snacks and supplies. Nicole would leave her cell phone number in big letters next to the phone, as the primary go-to person if Mom needed anything.

"I'll never be more than a half hour away, no matter what," Nicole said. So we worked out the details of what I would pay her. Nicole would keep track of her hours, and I would pay her at the end of each week, plus reimburse her for gas and any other expenses.

What could go wrong?

Mom was delighted when I told her that Nicole wanted to come see her every day and help around the house.

"Well, I could use help with my laundry," Mom said.

Mom thrived under Nicole's loving care. She was thrilled at the attention, she was always clean and well dressed, and she was eating more. Nicole liked to cook, so we plugged the stove back in, and Mom ate scrambled eggs or French toast for breakfast, toasted cheese sandwiches and tomato soup for lunch, and a salad or a bowl of oatmeal with berries for dinner.

One night in early February, a frigid blast of winter, gift from Canada by way of Lake Erie, closed most of the roads and left drifts in the driveways that made travel impossible. Nicole's rented house, a half hour from Mom's, was buried under two feet of snow. Fifteen miles south, we were snowed in, as was Gary, who lived 10 miles northwest of Mom on the shore of Lake Erie.

I called Nicole at 7 a.m. to see whether she could make it to Mom's early.

"I have four wheel drive," Nicole said. "I can try to get through. I worry about Grandma. She's probably scared all by herself."

"Let me call Grandma and see if she's okay," I said. "We can decide what to do after I talk to her. You get ready to go."

But when I dialed Mom's number, it just rang. Thinking maybe she was napping or in the bathroom, I tried again a few minutes later. No response. After the third try, I called Nicole, then Gary. Nicole assured me she would be able to get through and would let me know as soon as she reached Mom's.

111

Gary said he'd try to get through and dig a path for Nicole. I debated whether to start driving there myself, but Ed said to wait until we knew what was going on.

The next forty-five minutes seemed like hours. The clock's ticking became loud and annoying, as I glanced up at it every couple of minutes.

Finally, Gary called.

"It's not good," he said. "We managed to get into her driveway with Nicole's four wheel drive. The roads are a mess. And when we finally got here, the house was freezing, and Mom was on the floor in the upstairs hallway, in her nightgown. She must have fallen during the night when she got up to go to the bathroom. The ambulance is on its way. I hope they can get through. Nicole is with her, keeping her calm and warm. Mom's awake but seems out of it."

"I'm on my way," I told my brother.

"No," Gary said. "By the time you get here, we will probably be at the hospital. Meet us there. And be extra careful. Some of the roads are closed with downed trees and power lines."

"Why was the house cold?"

"Apparently, when Mom went to turn the thermostat down for the night, she turned the furnace totally off instead. I turned it back on, but it's still pretty cold in here. Temperature shows 52 degrees."

"Poor Mom! I wonder how long she was on the floor."

"No way to tell. She also has a nasty cut on her head. I think she must have done that when she fell," Gary said. "I need to hang up now and dig a path for the ambulance. See you at the hospital."

The main roads were open, but still treacherous, as Ed and I hurried to Lake West Hospital. We soon found Mom in the emergency room, with Gary, Pattie, and Nicole with her. Mom was sitting up in a hospital bed, with a hospital gown on, swaddled in blankets.

"Well, for cryin' out loud," she said when she saw us. "You didn't have to come all this way. It was just a little bump on the head. I'll be fine. You all don't need to make such a fuss. How did it happen, anyway? I don't remember a thing."

After a morning spent in X-rays, CAT scans, PET scans, blood tests, lab work, and exams by a variety of doctors, the verdict was that Mom needed staples for the gash on her head. No broken bones, but she had developed a full-blown urinary tract infection and was subsequently confused.

They kept Mom in the hospital for nine days. We all took turns staying with her. She slept most of the time, and was confused during her awake periods. She hummed constantly.

All of us were with her when a social worker asked to meet with us.

After confirming that I had power of attorney, and therefore could make decisions on Mom's behalf, the social worker put into words what we already knew but didn't want to face: that Mom was in the early stages of dementia, and would no longer be able to function on her own. Her head wound, bumps and bruises were all healing well, and her UTI was responding to antibiotics, but Mom was going to need physical therapy in a rehab facility for a number of weeks.

"We will recommend several places that take her insurance, and we will work with you to determine the best strategy for her care," she said, her tone sympathetic but businesslike.

She told us that the staff doctor had determined that Mom could no longer manage stairs, and would need almost constant supervision.

This would not be welcome news to Mom.

"Don't tell her yet," the social worker recommended. "Wait and see how she does in rehab."

"Mom is terrified of having to go into a nursing home," I told her. "We promised Dad when he passed away that we would keep her in their house as long as possible."

The social worker smiled. She had heard this before, many, many times.

"Well, we'll cross that bridge later," she said. "First let's get her into a rehab center and see how she does."

114

During the next few days, as the hospital planned Mom's release, the five of us visited the recommended rehab centers. The first was horrible, like something out of an Alfred Hitchcock movie. Dark halls smelling of urine and medicine, sad people with vacant eyes, slumped in their wheelchairs, impersonal attendants ignoring them.

We hurried out after ten minutes, as soon as we could politely thank the nurse for the tour.

"I can't believe this was on the recommended list," I said. "Mom wouldn't last a week in there. No way will we put our Mom in that terrible place."

The second facility on the list was better, but the attendants all appeared overworked and hurried. I crossed it off the list. At least it was clean and bright.

The third place, Maple Meadows, was the farthest away from all of us, but it had just opened. The craftsman-style facility was breathtaking, all stone and tile, with a massive fireplace and lovely furniture. The walls were covered with cheerful pastoral paintings of flowers, horses, and waterfalls.

We arrived at mealtime, and saw well-dressed, clean people, many of them in wheelchairs or using walkers, who were engaged in pleasant conversation. The food smelled delicious. Attendants bustled about, making sure everyone had what they needed.

We explained to the marketing officer, a pleasant lady named Julie, that we needed to find a temporary place for Mom, who needed physical and occupational therapy for a few weeks. Julie showed us the rooms, all cheerful, spacious, with private baths. They could take her immediately, she informed us. Mom's insurance would pay for everything for up to 30 days.

It sounded too good to be true. After a ten minute conference, we made the unanimous decision to have Mom transported there as soon as the hospital released her.

The next afternoon, I met the ambulance there at Maple Meadows, as two burly young men wheeled Mom in on a gurney, clutching her battered purse to her chest, her eyes wide with fear.

"Thank Heavens you're here!" Mom exclaimed. "I had no idea where they were taking me! I thought I was going home, but this isn't home! I want to go home! Take me home! I want to be in my own bed!"

"Hi, Mom," I said, kissing her on the cheek. "The doctor said you need to be here for awhile as you recover from your fall."

"What fall? I don't remember falling."

"You had a nasty fall a couple of weeks ago, and hurt your head," I explained. "You've been in the hospital ever since."

"No, I haven't, "Mom said, moving her head from side to side emphatically. "I don't remember any fall, or being in the hospital. What happened?"

As the attendants got her into a hospital bed in her new room, I explained, as gently as possible, the events of the last two weeks. She was amazed.

"Why don't I remember any of this?" she demanded.

"You've had an infection that made you confused," I said. "But you're better now. The doctor wants you to do some exercises to gain your strength while you are here."

"So when can I go home to my own bed?" she asked.

"When the doctor says it is okay," I said. "It depends on how well you do the exercises."

I visited Mom every day, mainly to reassure her that we knew where she was, and she was not alone. She responded well to the therapy, which included walking with a walker back and forth, and tossing a balloon to keep it in the air as long as possible.

"These are like kids' games," she giggled. "They're kind of fun, but I can't for the life of me figure how this is doing me any good."

"They know what they're doing, Mom," I said. "They went to college for this."

"Well, that was a big waste of good money," she said with a harrumph. "So when do you take me home?"

"As soon as the doctor says you're ready to function on your own."

Mom enjoyed the food. She sat at a table with three other ladies. I would often arrive at lunch time, to help her eat if needed.

"Fried chicken today," Mom told me. "With green beans, scalloped potatoes, and Jello for dessert. There's always room for Jello." She giggled at the old commercial.

"Looks good," I ventured.

"Want some?" Mom asked, proffering her filled fork. "Here, have a bite."

I obeyed, and told her it was delicious.

"Not as good as Mom's, or even as good as mine," Mom said. "Maybe I should go into the kitchen and show them how it's done."

"Maybe you should," I agreed, knowing full well it wasn't going to happen.

Mom picked up a slip of paper next to her plate, with her name and menu choice on it. She pulled her ancient purse from her lap.

"Time to pay the check," she said. "How much is it? I don't have my reading glasses."

"That's not a check, Mom," I said gently. "That's the menu that you mark every night before you go to bed."

Mom narrowed her eyes.

"I've never been to this restaurant before," she said. "Now let me pay the bill so I can go home. I'm tired and I need a nap in my own bed."

I took the "check" and pretended to pay it at the beverage bar. I helped her down the hall to her room.

"Hey, this isn't my house," she accused. "Where is my house? I want my own bed."

"This is just a room for naps after lunch," I reassured her.

"At the restaurant? Why, I've never heard of such a thing. But I am tired. Too tired to argue. Do you think anyone would mind if i just took a little rest for a few minutes?"

Every day it was the same. I would "surprise" her at lunch.

"Well, for cryin' out loud. How did you know how to find me at this restaurant?" she'd marvel, clutching her cracked leather pocketbook on her lap. We had taken out everything from her purse except a handkerchief, her plastic folding rain bonnet, a keychain with useless keys from Dad's old Lincoln, long gone, and her almost-empty wallet.

"Here's my credit card," she said, handing me her expired library card. "Go pay my bill, and include a nice tip. Maybe even 50 cents. I think I can afford that. Then take me home. I want to go to bed."

And every afternoon she would take a nice nap in the "restaurant's" nap room.

Just as Mom appeared to adapt to the routine at Maple Meadows, Kathy, the social worker, called me into her office one Wednesday.

"Lois is doing very well here, and she's definitely my favorite," Kathy said. "She's a sweetheart. But unfortunately, her insurance will run out at the end of the week, and we can't keep her any longer unless we transfer her to the nursing home wing."

Kathy told me the nursing home would cost us $8,500 a month. I mentally calculated how much was left in Mom's checking account, which was healthy but not loaded. I told Kathy I would get back to her.

Time for another committee meeting.

Over dinner at the local Cracker Barrel, we pondered our next step.

"Does Mom have enough money to pay for a nursing home?" Gary asked.

"Sure, but the question is, how long will she need it?" I said. "From my calculations, at $8,500 per month, there is enough in her account to pay for maybe six to eight years, depending on whether we need to sell the house. It all depends on how long she will still be with us. At this rate, given her physical health, she could last another ten years. "

"The house should be sold anyway," Ed said. "The maintenance, taxes, and insurance will eat up her money quickly."

"That will break her heart," I said. "Dad built that house for her when he got back from World War II. Except for the old homestead back in Missouri, it's the only home she has ever really known. It's never had a mortgage. It's always been in the family."

"I know, but it's just a house, after all," said Ed. Two pairs of eyes---half of them Gary's, the other half mine---stared at him in disbelief.

"Hon, that is so much more than just a house," I said, since it was my place to explain. "You have lived in lots of places, so you have no idea. It has been ingrained in us since we were babies: the house is our homestead, our heritage, built with Dad's own hands, board by board, and all of us were raised there. Mom and Dad always told us, over and over from the time we were little, that the house should always be in the family. Why, it's even had the same phone number since 1952 and the same stove since 1947."

"I know, I know, but I think you two are crazy," my beloved husband said. "What are you going to do with it? Make it a shrine to Jack and Lois? You can't possibly live there."

"As you know, since you wrote it, Mom's will specifies that Gary has first rights to the house after Mom passes," I explained. "If he wants it, he will buy my share, my half, when the time comes. I will get more cash from the estate, and Gary will get the house."

"If there's any cash left," Ed pointed out. "There might be just the house left, if Mom needs to be in a nursing home for a long length of time. You need to figure out what to do with the house."

"And, of course, I want it," Gary said.

"And I don't," I added. "So that works out just fine."

"The house will be the last to go," Gary said. I quietly nodded in agreement. Ed shot me a frustrated look, rolled his eyes, and raised his hands.

"I give up," he said.

Nicole said, "Listen. I have an idea. It would kill Grandma to have to leave the house that she and Grandpa built and have lived in and raised their family for almost 70 years. What if I move in with Grandma and take care of her? She likes me, and I take good care of her. I can live there rent free, and maybe you can pay me here and there. That way her money will last, she'll be taken care of, and she'll be in her own home as long as she can."

My relief was almost palpable. God bless Nicole.

So it was agreed, on a trial basis. Mom would have to be restricted to the first floor, which had no bedroom and only a half bath. She would miss her big king sized bed terribly, but we had no choice. The downstairs rooms were all too small to accommodate the big bed. We would rent a hospital bed for her and set it up in the dining room. We would put up a screen to give her as much privacy as possible.

Nicole would use the upstairs guest room. She volunteered to install nanny cameras throughout the downstairs, complete with night vision, so we could watch Mom on our phones when Nicole was away or not in the room.

So on a blustery St. Patrick's Day, 2015, an ambulance delivered Mom from Maple Meadows home to the beloved homestead she had lived in for seven decades.

She was ecstatic to walk in the back door, with her walker, and into her kitchen, where Nicole already had lunch on the table for her. Nicole had even bought a bouquet of pastel roses from the supermarket. Next to Mom's place was a small bowl of M&Ms and a box containing her favorite jigsaw puzzle.

"Oh, it's so good to be home," Mom said through tears. "That restaurant was nice, but I was afraid they would keep me there forever. They did have a comfy nap room, though."

After lunch came the first major hurdle of Mom's Next Chapter.

"I think I'll just go up to bed now," Mom said, as Nicole and I exchanged glances.

"Uh, Grandma," Nicole said. "We had to put a bed for you downstairs. The doctor said you can't go up and down stairs anymore."

"What? In my own house? Who says I can't get around in my own house? Why, that's ridiculous. I've been going up and down stairs here for seventy years."

"I know, Mom, but you had a terrible fall that put you in the hospital and a rehab center for several weeks. The doctor doesn't want you falling again," I ventured.

"In the hospital? Are you sure? That's funny. I don't remember falling, or being in the hospital, at all," she said, shaking her head in disbelief.

I gently touched the almost-healed scar on the back of her head, tangible proof of the last few months' situation.

I explained, as calmly as I could, that she had fallen and injured her head pretty badly, and had spent a scary night on the hall floor, in the cold, unable to get up. Gary had found her there and an ambulance had taken her to the hospital, where she had been for several days with a serious infection. The doctor had ordered her sent to a rehab center, where she had spent three weeks recovering.

"Three WEEKS?!! You're kidding!" she exclaimed. "Why don't I remember any of this?"

"I think it was very scary, and traumatic," I replied. "You were very sick, and a lot of people were worried about you. The doctor doesn't want a repeat performance, so he told us that if we insisted on taking you home, you would have to stay on the first floor."

"But my bedroom, and clothes, and the bathroom are all on the second floor," Mom whined. It was painful to see the disbelief and worry in the deep lines of her wrinkled face.

"Couldn't I get one of those chairs that takes you up and down the stairs?" she asked. "I've seen them on TV."

"I looked into that," I told her. "They are very expensive, and your stairway is too narrow for it. Besides, the doctor said it would be next to impossible to manage it on your own. Getting on and off would be dangerous."

Mom blew her nose and started to cry in earnest. My heart bled for her. Mom had never been dependent, let alone helpless, in her whole life. She was always the one to look out for elderly neighbors, taking them to doctors' appointments, getting their groceries for them, and even cleaning their houses for them (although she'd usually volunteered me for that job).

Nicole helped her to the bathroom, then tucked her into the hospital bed we had set up in the dining room. We had moved the maple Early American dining table and chairs onto the sun porch and had cleared Mom's knick-knack collections from the hutch and the corner cupboard. We had set up a small TV and remote on the hutch, added room-darkening drapes, and set up a potty chair in case the walk to the bathroom would be too long some night.

Gary bought a locking, clear plastic cover for the thermostat, located in the dining room, so Mom would no longer be tempted to turn off the heat.

Also hidden on the hutch was a tiny surveillance camera, one of four set up on the first floor. We could see virtually everything on the first floor with the rotating cameras, even in the pitch dark. Nicole and I could monitor Mom's every move at any time of the day or night from our phones, so Nicole could watch her from the upstairs guestroom and I could watch from my house. I felt a bit sneaky spying on my mother like that, but it couldn't be helped.

"I don't like this at all," Mom groused from the new bed. "I want my own bed. This is ridiculous that I can't sleep in my own bed."

"I know, Mom, and I totally sympathize," I said. "But the doctor didn't want you to come home at all. This was our compromise. You can stay in your house if you stay on the first floor. We are trying this to see how it goes."

"What happens if I don't like it?" she asked.

I took a deep breath, dreading having to say the terrible words that strike terror in the hearts of elderly people everywhere.

"If this doesn't work out, the doctor said you will have to go to a nursing home."

I can tell you, seeing your mother sob uncontrollably is enough to break the most stoic heart.

Chapter Eleven

"Take me to my bed."

November 14, 2015

Under Nicole's loving care, Mom thrived throughout the spring, summer, and fall. Most of her days were spent doing endless jigsaw puzzles at the kitchen table, or easy crosswords from paperback books piled on the end table next to her torture chamber chair.

Mentally, she wasn't improving, but she also wasn't degenerating either. In a person with dementia, that's a big plus, almost like progress. There were days when her mind was relatively clear, when she enjoyed reading Dad's old letters to her from World War II, or pouring over album after album of old black and white photos, some going back to her growing-up days on the family farm in Missouri.

She especially treasured an 8x10 photo taken in about 1924 on the front porch of her uncle's large block house on Jakes Prairie, just up the dirt road from her family homestead.

Uncle Joe had built the house himself from blocks made from a cement-like material mixed on the banks of the nearby Bourbois River, in molds he had bought from the Sears catalog. For his mother's 85th birthday, family from as far away as St. Louis had gathered to honor her, and all forty of them had gathered on the front porch for the first-ever, and last, family photo.

Mom treasured her copy of that photo, and would trot it out for every visitor who ever came through her door.

"Did I ever show you this?" she would ask for the 750th time. Of course, we would always say no.

She would recite the names, one by one, of loved ones now long gone, but their image captured forever by a professional photographer brought all the way from St. James to chronicle the occasion.

The 751st time I saw the photo, it dawned on me that Mom, a tiny, undersized, tow-headed five-year-old seated on the bottom step in the center of the photo, was the last of that entire group still living.

Another thing about Alzheimer's is that the person loses their short term memory, but their long term memory remains pretty much intact. Mom might struggle to remember the name of Nicole, her granddaughter and care giver, but she could identify her five siblings and dozens of aunts, uncles, cousins, and other kinfolk in a photograph taken almost a century ago.

Mom was holding her own mentally, although it was a case of two steps forward and one step back, followed by one step forward and two steps back. Some days she was relatively sharp, but the next day, or sometimes even the next hour, she struggled to remember my name.

"Do you know who I am?" I'd sometimes quiz her.

"Of course I do, silly," she'd laugh. "I gave birth to you."

"So what's my name?"

"Sweetie," she'd say. "Sweetie" was her designation for anyone whose name she couldn't remember at the moment. She thought she was hiding the fact that she couldn't summon the name. We usually didn't correct her, to her satisfaction that she had pulled another one over on us. But sometimes, out of frustration, we would tell her the right name.

"Diane. Of course. I knew that. You didn't have to tell me," she would say in a huff.

Gary decided to make a game out of it.

"My name is Ghengis Khan," he'd tell her.

"No it isn't," Mom would say. "It's Sweetie."

"George Washington?"

"Nobody made you the father of our country. You can't fool me. I know who you are."

"So who am I?" Gary would ask.

"You're my brother," Mom would announce, nodding in satisfaction that she had figured it out.

"But what's my name?"

Mom would ponder for a few seconds, followed by a little sigh.

"Sweetie," she'd finally guess. Then the rocking and the hummmmmm hummmmmm HMMMM-ing would start, signaling GAME OVER.

The nanny cams were a godsend and a curse at the same time. I studied Mom's behavior, especially late at night, trying to learn her patterns, if there were any.

Mom was restless in the hospital bed. Nicole would put her in her nightgown and tuck her into bed before going out or going up to the guestroom, but within a half hour, Mom was up, with her walker, making her way slowly to the stairs, a determined, almost angry, expression on her face.

She would set the walker aside and try once again, and once again in vain, to unfasten the baby gate blocking the stairs. Gary had found a complicated one at Home Depot---a tall one that was virtually impossible to unlock without the secret latch. Nicole could step over it easily, but Mom couldn't.

Mom would fuss with the gate for several minutes. I would then cringe to see her lift her leg as high as she could get it, using both hands, and try to go over the top of the gate.

She would give up after several tries. Sometimes she would lie down on the living room couch; other times she would squeeze into the small, back- torturing, rocking love seat in the TV room.

Once she lay down on the floor out of frustration, to my shock and dismay.

After a few minutes, she reached up onto her chair and pulled down a small pillow and an ancient, faded green-and-brown woolen afghan we had given her for Christmas in 1978. She put her head on the pillow, wrapped the afghan around her, and fell into a deep sleep. I turned on the volume and heard her snoring loudly. Well, at least she was asleep.

Nicole was out with friends that evening and had not yet arrived home, so I watched Mom for the next several minutes.

After a half hour, she stirred and struggled to sit up. She scooted slowly on her backside, over to her padded torture chamber rocking chair, and tried in vain to pull herself up.

I dialed Gary.

"Yeah, I see her," my brother said. "I don't know where Nicole is. She's not answering her phone. I'll head on over to Mom's and get her back to bed."

I continued to watch Mom, who had fallen back asleep, her back up against her chair. She didn't seem to be in any pain or distress. Within 20 minutes, the kitchen light came on, and then the light in the TV room, as Gary walked into the room. He waved at the camera to tell me he had arrived.

"So why are you on the floor, Mom?" Gary asked, as Mom opened her eyes.

"Well, for cryin' out loud; what are you doing here?" Mom asked.

"I'm here to put you back to bed."

"How did you know where to find me?"

"I'm psychic," he told her.

"Help me up so I can go to bed," Mom commanded. "In my own bed. I can't sleep in the dining room. I want my own bed."

"You are not allowed to go upstairs; doctor's orders," Gary told her. "You keep falling, and I'm getting tired of finding you on the floor."

"I've never been on the floor," Mom insisted.

"You're on the floor now," Gary said, holding her shoulders and gently lifting her up.

"Well, either you help me upstairs to my bed or I'll walk up there myself," Mom groused. "One way or the other, I'm going to sleep in my own bed."

"No, you're not."

"Yes, I will, and you can't stop me," Mom said, heading for the stairs, blocked by the baby gate.

Just then, the back door opened and Nicole entered the room.

"What's going on, Dad?" she asked. "Is Grandma okay?"

"I'm going to bed, upstairs, and nobody can stop me," Mom told her.

"No, you're not," Nicole insisted. "Sit in your chair until you calm down."

"I am perfectly calm," Mom said, lowering herself into her torture chair. "But I need to sit down, just for a minute. Then I'M GOING TO BED or I'm calling the police and telling them you are holding me hostage."

Whew. I was glad we'd finally discontinued the landline last month.

"Go ahead and call the police," Gary said, aware that there was no longer a working dial phone in the house. "They will see a crazy woman raving at her kids and refusing to go to bed. They will call an ambulance and have you taken to the hospital."

"What for? I'm perfectly fine," Mom said. "Except for being held hostage in my own house."

"It's called a change in mental status," Gary said. "They can keep you overnight for observation. Then maybe everybody will be able to get some sleep."

"You wouldn't dare."

"Try me," Gary said. "I was raised to be as stubborn as you."

Nicole cajoled her into walking with her into the dining room, with the promise of a bowl of M&Ms. She sweetened the pot with an offer of a Little Debbie.

"Well, okay; for you, Sweetie, I'll do it, just this once, but not for that brother of mine over there," Mom said, glaring at her son. "He always was the stubborn one."

Within 20 minutes, Mom was sound asleep in the hospital bed. Gary turned out the lights, except for the nightlights, waved goodbye to the camera, and therefore to me, told me he'd call me in the morning, and tiptoed out.

Nicole sat in a folding chair next to the hospital bed and watched Mom snore for another half hour, then went upstairs to her room. She whispered to the camera before she left the dining room, "I'll watch her from my room. You go ahead and get some sleep."

I watched Mom until about 2 a.m., till my eyes drooped and dreams started invading my thoughts.

"It's about time you came to bed," Ed said as I climbed in beside him. "You're watching those cameras 24/7, worse than store security. You need your sleep too."

I wasn't about to argue.

One good thing about Alzheimer's is every day is a do-over. The next day, Mom had no memory of the previous night's trauma.

As an early Christmas present, I bought Mom a reclining lift chair that I'd found on buy-sell-trade online. A nice lady in Willowick, about 10 miles away, told me she had bought it for her father, who had refused to sit in it.

"He wouldn't sit in anything except his ratty old platform rocker," the lady said. "He passed away three weeks ago, and I have no need for this."

So we made arrangements for Gary to borrow a pick-up truck, and the following Saturday, he, Ed, and Nicole loaded it into the truck's bed and made the trip to Mom's.

"Well, for cryin' out loud," Mom said. "Why is everybody here?"

"We have a surprise for you," I told her. I took her into the living room while everybody took out the old torture chamber chair, brought in the new lift chair, and set it up.

Mom was skeptical at first, naturally.

"There's nothing wrong with my old rocker," she said. "Dad bought it for me and it just fits this small room."

"Mom, you've complained for years how your back hurts when you sit in the rocker," I said. "Nobody else can sit in it at all. This chair is so comfortable you'll even be able to sleep in it, and it raises and lowers with the push of a button. "

After five or six lifts up and down with the remote, Mom conceded that the chair was, indeed, very comfortable, and fun to operate.

"So what will you do with MY chair?" she asked.

One more time, I lied to my parent.

"Gary's going to work on it," I said. "The arm's gotten loose, and needs repair."

"So when do I get it back?" she asked, suspicion creeping into her voice.

"As soon as I fix it," my brother lied.

Mom soon discovered that although the new chair was no substitute for her bed, it was a close second in comfort. She slept in it many nights from then on. Another problem solved, at least for now.

Chapter Twelve

"I found my Cherry Kiss."

April 4, 2016

Mom continued to decline, slowly but steadily. Nicole, the most stubborn of us all in a family known for its rock-headedness, considered it a challenge to keep Mom going as long as possible in her own house, but as time went on, that was looking more difficult every day.

We had swapped Mom's underwear with adult diapers during the winter, when she started having accidents. Nicole didn't mind changing her, and often changing Mom's slacks as well, and I did the laundry more frequently.

Mom tried to take care of her bathroom needs, but as time went on, she simply forgot. This was the woman who had potty trained me, not to mention, all three of us.

Once when I was there, she had an accident. When I asked her to stand so I could clean her, she leaked again, with feces landing everywhere. I cleaned her, put clean slacks on her, and washed the floor, baseboards, and wherever else needed it.

Mom, thankfully, was oblivious to it all. Soon, she was back in her recliner, watching the Cleveland Indians' opening day on TV, humming her standard hum.

In previous years, Mom kept track of each player, the score, the inning, and the important plays. She had her favorite players, and cheered them when they came up to bat. She had special nicknames for her very favorites.

She called Asdrubal Cabrera "Pearlie" because of the beads he wore around his neck. He had been her favorite for the last year or two.

This opening day, however, she just stared vacantly at the screen, humming. When Nicole came in, she told me that Grandma had seemed out of it since yesterday afternoon.

"How's the game going, Grandma?" Nicole asked her.

"Who's playing?" Mom asked. "I haven't been paying attention."

"It's opening day, Mom," I said. "You always look forward to opening day."

"They're playing in January?" Mom asked, amazed.

"No, Mom, it's April," I said gently.

"April showers bring May flowers," Mom pointed out, giggling. "It's raining, it's pouring, the old man is snoring."

She chuckled and began to hum, "April in Paris."

Hoo boy.

Late that night, when Nicole was out with friends, Mom woke up about 1 a.m. She wandered around the house, opening drawers, apparently in search of something. On the nanny cam I saw her place some small item in her left hand and close her fist over it.

She tottered from the living room into the small TV room, and began examining herself in the mirror. She grimaced, made a face at herself, then slowly made her way around the room, holding onto the furniture as she went. She straightened one of the curtains, picked up the internet router, examined it closely with a puzzled look on her face, then noticed the nanny cam sitting next to it.

She picked up the tiny globe-shaped camera and stared at it, twisting it this way and that. I could see one big eye with a curious expression, and began to get dizzy as she twisted the camera with mild curiosity but no apparent recognition. I was relieved when she set the camera back down.

After several minutes, still in the dark, she opened her left hand and transferred something to her right hand. She pulled at a tubular object, removed the top, twisted the bottom, and raised it to her mouth.

With heavy concentration, humming her rhythmic hmmmmmm hmmmmmmm HMMMMM, hmmmmmmm hmmmmm HMMMMM, she painted her lips and the surrounding area with her favorite Cherry Kiss lipstick, then stared at the camera. She took the lipstick once more, and slowly painted her cheeks, forehead, eyelids, and neck with it, with long up-and-down strokes.

Still humming, she touched the lipstick to her left shoulder and ran it up and down her arm. By the time she reached the fingertips on her left hand, Nicole entered the room.

"What did you DO, Grandma?" she asked Mom, in a frustrated-parent voice.

"Pretty. Pretty. Pretty. You're a pretty girl, Sweetie," Mom said, giggling.

Nicole spent the next half hour washing the bright red lipstick off of Mom and putting her back to bed. She took the remains of the lipstick case upstairs with her as soon as Mom was asleep. She wouldn't chance throwing it away downstairs, where Mom could find it and retrieve it.

The next morning, Nicole told me that Mom had opened all the faucets, in the kitchen and half bath, wide open and let the water run full blast downstairs all night as Nicole slept upstairs. Thank God the drains were all working.

I did a group text with Ed, Gary, Pattie, and Nicole.

It's time, was all I said.

Chapter Thirteen

"My daughter hears a choir of angels."

May 10, 2016

The internet is the greatest invention known to man. In previous years, I would have pulled out the Yellow Pages and looked under NURSING HOMES. I would have made a list and called each one to schedule a visit.

But thanks to Google, I quickly found the websites for several assisted living facilities with memory care wings, all within a close radius of Mom's house. I prayed for guidance, and somehow was directed to Sunnybrook, an "independent retirement community" about a mile away. Next door was Sunset Place, an assisted living with a "life guidance" wing.

All the reviews were glowing, with an overall rating of 4.8 out of 5.

 It sounded like a good place to start my search. I called and made an appointment for that afternoon with Jeanne, the marketing director.

Jeanne was in her 50s, matronly and pleasant, and we hit it off immediately. I explained our situation to her as I sat in her office, sipping from the small bottle of cold water she had offered me.

"This is an amazing coincidence," Jeanne said. "Our life guidance wing has only one double-sized room,

142

which at the moment is the same price as a single room. The family who had reserved it for their mom and dad changed their minds this morning, so it's available right now. You bring your own furniture. If you want it, it's yours, but you will need to decide today because it will be snapped up immediately by somebody else if you don't. It's the best room we have.

At first I thought Jeanne had held an earlier career as a car salesman, because that spiel was so old it had whiskers. Take action now, and sign on the dotted line. An opportunity like this doesn't come along every day. If you don't snap it up, somebody else will and you'll regret it.

It was worth a shot. It didn't cost anything to look.

Jeanne took me on a tour of the main assisted living facility, beginning with the huge main lobby, where a programmed piano softly played Rogers and Hammerstein's greatest show tunes.

"Oh, what a beautiful morning..." it plinked merrily.

A massive stone fireplace, unlit, graced one wall. Overstuffed chairs were occupied by about a dozen people, and in one corner, four were concentrating on a game of mah jong at a square oak table. The plastic tiles clicked, as the players ignored everything else around them.

Across the hall, the main dining room was filled with people seated at tables for four. The soft clink of china dishes and the buzz of conversations made a pleasant scene. Laughter sprinkled the room like

143

dappled sunlight, as attendants served dishes with aromas that reminded me I had missed breakfast.

"The memory care wing is down here," Jeanne said, leading me down a long corridor with matching pastel floral wreaths gracing double doors at one end. A key pad sat on the wall next to the door. Jeanne quickly keyed in a series of numbers.

"We change the code every other day," she explained. "Our clients are very vulnerable, of course, and must be protected 24/7."

The memory unit was bright, sunny, and beautifully decorated. A black metal "Welcome" sign in script sat on a low divider separating the entryway from a dining room, not nearly as grand as the one in the main section. Tables for four dotted the room, but here the conversation was much less lively.

About a dozen attendants helped two dozen residents finish lunch. The residents, some in wheel chairs, some with walkers, and a few with four-pronged canes, all looked clean and well dressed, and were bent over small dishes of ice cream, concentrating on their dessert and oblivious to the visitors.

The place smelled fresh, with a slight, pleasant, citrus scent. There seemed to be plenty of staff members, all smiling, gently leading people to the bathroom or back to their rooms as they finished their ice cream.

One tall elderly lady walked up and down the hallway pushing an old-fashioned carpet sweeper, a determined look on her face.

144

"Good morning, Mary," Jeanne said to her. "How is your job going today?"

"This place is a mess," Mary groused. "People just don't care about being neat, and they leave everything for me to clean up. I have four more rooms to clean. It never ends."

Jeanne whispered, "Mary thinks she works here, so we gave her the carpet sweeper for something to do. We try to find each client's happy spot and play along. It helps keep anxiety to a minimum."

At one table in the dining room, another lady, probably in her late 80s, tried to feed a spoonful of ice cream to a realistic-looking baby doll seated on her lap. She was crooning "Rock a Bye, Baby." The doll didn't respond.

"That's Annabel," Jeanne explained. "Dolly is the only thing that keeps her calm. We have to make sure that another client doesn't think it's hers and take it from her."

A tall man in his late 60s, wearing Cleveland Browns sweats and a Vietnam Veteran ball cap, stood by the door with studied casualness.

"Bill is always trying to escape," Jeanne whispered. "He stays by the door and tries to slip out when people come in or out. He wants to go home. Of course he does, but his home is here, and has been for two years."

Five women and three men, apparently already finished with lunch, sat in comfortable chairs around

145

a large TV in a common living room attached to the dining room, some watching a colorful program on tropical fish, while others nodded off in their after-lunch nap.

One lady, with a walker, struggled in vain to open a French door that led to a sunny courtyard garden.

"Betty, it's a little chilly to be outside today, don't you think? Maybe later," Jeanne said, as an attendant took Betty by the hand and gently guided her toward the living room.

Leaving the central common area, we walked down a corridor with an outside door at the end. Jeanne stopped at one door labeled MODEL UNIT #1, selected a key from several on a large key ring, opened a door, and motioned me inside.

The sunny, cheerful room was small, and divided into two tiny sections, each with a single bed, and small dresser topped with a tiny TV.

"This is our most basic room," she explained. "It has two beds and a shared bath with a walk-in shower.'

 I told her Mom would never be able to handle having a roommate.

"I know. I just wanted to show you all the options," she told me as she unlocked the door of MODEL UNIT #2, a standard single room. It was bright, clean, and nicely appointed, but still a little small. It wouldn't fit even a double bed, let alone a king.

"So here's the one I was telling you about," Jeanne said, at the door of a room at the end of the hall, right next to an exit, labeled MODEL UNIT #3. She noted my quizzical expression at the location.

"Don't worry; no one can get in or out that door unless it's a true emergency and we buzz it open," Jeanne assured me. "Alarms will sound. We are very secure in this wing. We have to be. The only way in or out is the big door near the dining room, although each corridor has an emergency exit, and there are many doors opening into the central, secure, interior courtyard.

When she opened the door to the big, sunny room, I could almost hear the heavenly choir singing as they held a banner proclaiming THIS IS IT!

The room had huge windows on three sides, and it was big enough to fit a king sized bed, lift chair, TV, and dresser. I could already picture where the various pieces of Mom's furniture would go. It had a large en suite bathroom with walk-in shower and plenty of closet space.

After almost a year of struggling with hospital beds, Mom could sleep in her own bed at last.

"Where do I sign?" was all I said.

Chapter Fourteen

"I found my missing bed at last."

May 18, 2016

We had to hatch an elaborate plan to get Mom out of the house she had lived in for 70 years, 56 of them with Dad, and into a new chapter of her life at age 96. This wasn't going to be easy, because it was next to impossible to trick the ever-suspicious Mom.

After all the paper work was completed and a large check (room deposit and first month's expenses) written, I called a hasty meeting of our committee: Ed, Gary, Pattie, and Nicole at the local coffee shop. The latter three were a little surprised that I had made the decision so quickly, and without them, but when I showed them the photos on my phone, they understood.

"This is beautiful," Pattie said. "Look at all the natural light. Mom will like that."

"And it's so big," Gary contributed. "That's the biggest nursing home room I have ever seen."

"That's why I had to jump on it immediately," I explained. "She can sleep in her own bed again. I think this is probably the only room anywhere that could accommodate a king sized bed. It has been heartbreaking to see how desperately she wants to be in the bed that she and Dad shared for so many years. I think that represents 'home' and security to her."

"So how much is this costing us?" my ever-practical husband asked. "They undoubtedly will charge more for the bigger room."

"That's the best part," I assured everyone. "It doesn't cost any more than a standard single room. I don't know why it's that way, but we'll take it. It's the only double room in the place."

"So how much?" Ed asked. "Tax, title, and out the door."

"$6,500 a month total, for the room and Mom's care."

"Yikes," Nicole said. "Does Grandma have enough money to pay for it?"

I pointed out that the nursing home section of Maple Meadows was $8,500 a month, and the other places I had researched online ranged from $6,000 to $10,000. At the rate of $6,500, given Mom's bank accounts and investments, she could stay there for seven years, maybe eight, depending on whether we needed to sell her house.

"What happens if she outlives her money?" Gary asked. "We have no idea how long she has, but she may live to be 100, or even more, which would be wonderful. What happens then?"

"We all chip in, or she moves in with one of us," Ed said. The room went silent.

"So in other words, you and I might have to come up with $3,000 to $4,000 a month, every month, at some point," Gary said to me quietly.

"Unless she would qualify for Medicaid by then," Ed said. "But she would have to go somewhere else that takes Medicaid."

I shuddered at the picture of sad, helpless people in wheelchairs, lining dark, smelly hallways. No. I would take her to our house and take care of her myself, somehow, before subjecting Mom to that.

"I think it's horrible that we have to worry about how much longer Grandma will live," Nicole sniffed.

"But that's the reality of it," I said. "Grandpa left her in good financial shape, thank God, but the funds will eventually run out. Ed has been able to invest the money and make a nice income for Mom, but we have to plan as though that income won't be there, as we sell off the investments over time."

"It used to frustrate me, that Dad was always so careful with their money, that they did without things they needed, but now I see why he insisted on investing instead of spending," Gary said.

"Yes, I remember telling Dad to take Mom on a cruise, or buy a new car, or even to get Mom's teeth fixed," I said. "He wouldn't hear of it. He was always the frugal Scotsman. Thank God he was."

The room went silent again.

We decided to drive over to Sunset Place so everyone could see the room.

"This is gorgeous!" Pattie exclaimed. "We were very lucky to get this."

"I'm glad you think so, since I signed the contract so quickly without consulting everybody. I really thought there wasn't time," I said. "I couldn't risk losing it."

"Can we put our name on the waiting list for you and me?" Ed joked. "This is great. I could be very comfortable here. You did right to grab it."

We met with Jeanne in a small conference room. We decided on a move-in date of May 28, and she gave us the name of Eldercare Movers, a small local company that specialized in moving small amounts of furniture into, and out of, nursing homes and assisted living facilities. She estimated that the move would cost us about $200.

"I could borrow a pick-up truck and ask for volunteers," Gary said.

"No, we're too old to be moving furniture," I insisted. "We'll pay professionals."

Then came the big question. How on earth will we get Mom out of the house and over to Sunset Place? And, more important, how would we manage to explain to her why we were taking her out of her home of seven decades?

151

Worst of all, how would we deal with the guilt of having to break our promise to Dad, and break our mother's heart?

This was not going to be easy.

May 28 dawned warm and sunny. Mom's flowers were budding in her garden, and birds were announcing the news of the day in the bird world. Mom and Dad, avid bird watchers, would have been able to distinguish which type of birds were singing, if Dad were still alive and Mom able to hear.

Every year, during the first week of May, they would watch the newly-cleaned wren house hanging low on an apple tree in the back yard, and listen intently for the distinctive chirping warble. Each time the wrens made their presence known, usually around May 8, it was a cause for celebration.

I heard the wrens singing, and was surprised to find my eyes wet. Mom could no longer hear them, and undoubtedly had no memory of what they once meant to her and Dad anyway.

Sigh.

And I, their oldest child and only daughter, was there in the driveway on this beautiful day to remove my mother, by trick, from the home my parents built with their own hands, never to return.

I texted Ed: I'M HERE.

He responded immediately: I'M TWENTY MINUTES OUT. I'LL CIRCLE THE BLOCK IF YOUR CAR'S STILL THERE. I'LL LET THE OTHERS KNOW. GOOD LUCK.

"Well, for cryin' out loud. What are you doing here?" Mom asked as I walked in the back door.

"It's a beautiful day, and I'm going to put flags and flowers on the graves today, since Memorial Day is coming up soon," I told her, holding out one of the small flags.

"Now, where is Dad buried?" Mom asked. "He should have a flag."

"Dad was cremated, and his ashes scattered at your favorite vacation spot, up on the mountain in West Virginia," I told her. "Instead of a grave, we had a brick inscribed with his name and placed in the walk at the rose garden up on Mentor Avenue. Every year I put a tiny flag next to his brick. It's probably illegal to do that, but nobody seems to mind."

"I didn't know that," Mom said. "Or did I?"

"It was your idea," I told her. "Would you like to see it?"

"No, I never go out," Mom said, folding her arms.

"It's such a beautiful day," I told her. "The sun is shining, the flowers are blooming, and the birds are singing. Come on. It'll do you good to get out. Just for a little ride. I'll bring you right back."

Guilt stabbed me like an ice pick, right in the conscience. Mom had apparently lost her uncanny

153

ability to detect my lies. She was no longer a human polygraph.

Eventually, to my surprise and great relief, Mom relented. She went through the ritual of finding her purse and keys, and going to the bathroom. I helped her into the car, and texted Ed a hasty: WE'RE OFF.

As we made the turn onto Mentor Avenue, I spotted, through the rearview mirror, Nicole's car pulling into Mom's driveway behind us. So far, so good.

The rose garden was about a half mile away, within easy walking distance of Mom's house, but she couldn't walk that far anymore. I took my time driving, needing to stretch this trip as long as possible, to give Ed, Nicole, and the movers time to pack up Mom's bed, dresser, TV, lift chair, lamps, and end table. The movers were scheduled for 10:30 a.m. sharp, and everything depended on timing.

Ed would supervise the movers and follow them over to Sunset Place, directing them where to place everything.

Nicole would pack up some changes of clothes and essentials, including Mom's photo blanket, bedding, her Bible, the big family photo, and the photo of Grandma. Anything else she would need, we would bring over later.

It helped that Sunset Place was less than a mile away. Once the truck was packed, the actual move would take about a half hour.

"Well, that was real nice," Mom said as I helped her back into the car, slowly. "I didn't realize we had bricks there for Dad and Ken. I sure do miss them."

She wiped a few tears away with a kleenex from her purse and blew her nose. "Okay. I'm ready to go home now."

"Hey, I have an idea," I said. "Why don't we take some flowers to Grandma and Grandpa's grave?"

My grandparents were buried in the next town, about 15 minutes away. If I drove slowly, I could stretch the whole trip to an hour, giving the movers plenty of time, and giving Gary and Pattie time to get a bucket of chicken and set up a lunch in the small private dining room at Sunset Place.

After some initial reluctance, Mom's innate curiosity won out.

"I figured Mom and Pop must be dead by now, but where are they buried?" she asked.

"I'll show you."

"Why don't I know where it is?"

"You were the one who made the arrangements at the time, and you've been there many times," I replied. "You just don't remember. I'll take you there and you'll remember it immediately, I'm sure. It's not far."

On the way to the cemetery, I made the car do an unaccustomed crawl along Mentor Avenue, stretching the time as much as I could by pointing out

155

landmarks, such as my old elementary school, my high school, Mom's high school (class of 1937), and the site of the former factory where Dad worked.

"I've seen enough," Mom said. "I'm tired and would like to go home now."

I looked at my watch. Only a half hour gone. I needed more delay.

We visited Grandma and Grandpa's grave. Mom found it difficult to walk the short but unlevel grassy area from the car to the grave. She gripped my hand like a vise.

"Why did you put this big stone here?" Mom demanded, as she leaned on a huge black gravestone that I had never seen before, about a dozen feet from Grandma and Grandpa's grave.

"Wasn't me, Mom," I answered. "That's new since I was here last, about a year ago."

I laid the flowers on Grandma and Grandpa's grave.

"Remember when we would plant geraniums here every spring?" I asked Mom.

"Whose grave is this?" she demanded.

After explaining it again, I helped her back to my car and handed her an open bottle of water.

"Okay, time to go home," Mom announced, between sips, as she clutched her purse to her chest. I glanced at my watch. Why were the hands moving so slowly?

"Since we're here, why don't we drive past your old house?" I suggested.

We drove past both houses where Mom's family had lived, then the elementary school she had attended, her best friend's house, the storefront where she had first worked as a beautician, the family's church, the city hall where Dad had designed the electrical wiring in 1964, and the office space that had once been occupied by the family doctor. I got a lump in my throat when I realized she was seeing all these places for the last time, but she was unaware that she was saying goodbye to cherished memories.

"I really need to get home now, get some lunch, and take my nap," Mom said, in her best I'M THE MOM, YOU'RE THE CHILD voice.

"Wow! Would you look at that! I'm almost out of gas!" I declared, hoping she didn't notice the big "F" reading on my gas gauge. I pulled into a gas station, put the nozzle into my gas tank, and pumped $3 worth into the car in about as many seconds.

That used to buy a whole tank full. Now it's barely a gallon.

I walked a little distance from the pump and called Ed.

"Mom really wants to go home," I told him. "Have the movers finished?"

"They just arrived at the nursing home," he said. "You need to delay some more. How far away are you?"

"About ten minutes, tops," I said.

After I hung up, I chanced walking into the gas station's mini-mart, to kill a few more minutes. I couldn't risk her deciding to leave the car, so that used up maybe five. I bought two more bottles of water, a Little Debbie, and a pack of M&Ms for Mom, using up five more minutes.

"Why is this taking so long?" Mom demanded. "I'm getting hungry, and am really tired. Take me home. NOW."

"How about going out to lunch?" I suggested, my desperation rising, my voice shrill.

"No. I NEED TO GO HOME," she demanded. "NOW! Either take me home, or call a taxi for me."

"READY OR NOT. HERE WE COME," I texted Ed.

Ten minutes later, I pulled into Sunset Place. I could see Mom's furniture entering the main door and the moving truck parked right in front of us. I prayed that Mom wouldn't recognize her possessions being carried in, one by one.

Gary met us at the car door with a wheel chair.

"Well for cryin' out loud! How did you find us?" Mom asked. "Where are we, and what are you doing here?"

"Surprise!" he said. "The whole family is having lunch here. And you're the guest of honor."

"Why? Is it my birthday?" Mom asked.

I told Mom we just decided to surprise her. Gary helped her out of the car and into the wheelchair. Jeanne introduced herself to Mom and escorted us into the small private dining room, where Pattie, Nicole, and her sisters Kelly and Jessie had set the table with KFC chicken with all the trimmings, a cake, and balloons.

Mom was so overwhelmed that she didn't ask any more questions. As we seated her, Ed appeared, greeted Mom, and motioned to me that he was going back to the room to finish with the movers. He mouthed, "ALMOST DONE" as he left.

"Where's Ed going?" Mom asked.

"Bathroom," I lied.

Ten minutes later, Ed re-appeared, giving me the thumbs-up high sign. Mom had finished her chicken, potato salad, and green beans and was starting on her cake.

"This is quite a party," she said. "But I'm really tired now. Can I go home and go to bed?"

"Sure, Mom, just as soon as everyone is finished."

"Okay," she agreed.

As Ed wolfed down a chicken breast and the girls cleaned up the table, Mom's eyes closed and her head dropped onto her chest. The guilt hit me hard, since it was time now for Zero Hour.

Ed wheeled her down the hall, as I held her hand, Gary and family alongside. Jeanne buzzed us into the

159

memory care wing and stopped in front of the door to her new, probably final, home.

"Where are we going?" Mom asked. "It says LOIS on the door. This room must belong to another woman named Lois, who has the same name as me."

"No, Mom, this is the surprise," I said, more cheerful than I felt. "This is your room!"

"You mean they have a room for me at this restaurant?" she marveled.

"So you can take a nap," I lied, nodding like a bobblehead, as Pattie opened the door and Ed wheeled Mom in.

We weren't even fully into the room when Mom screeched, in a voice she hadn't used since she'd won a week's worth of groceries at the gas station in 1955, "MY BED!"

She leaped out of the still-moving wheelchair and dashed across the room like it was the 50 yard sprint in the Olympics. With one quick movement, she pulled back her pastel striped bedspread, jumped between her favorite flannel sheets, and fell back onto her pillow.

She was asleep before she landed, a huge, contented smile on her face.

I removed her shoes and tucked her in, as I took a quick glance around the cheerful room. It strongly resembled her bedroom at home, from the welcoming bed to the family photos on her dresser,

160

to the framed wedding picture, her Bible, and the photo of Grandma on the night stand next to her bed.

Ed had not left out any details. In the bathroom, her robe was hanging on a hook, and her worn, favorite monogrammed towels were hanging on the towel bar.

In the living room part of the suite, her photo blanket sat folded neatly over the back of her lift chair, and the TV remote sat on the end table, along with a small vase of fresh flowers. At that moment, my face leaked, part relief, part guilt, and part gratitude at what Ed had done to make the room feel like home for Mom.

Jeanne motioned everyone out in the hall, and we all tiptoed out of the room.

"She'll be fine now," she told us. "We can take it from here. It will be best for your mom if you leave her here for the next couple of days without visiting her. We'll call you if we need you. I think you will be surprised, when you see her, about how well she has adjusted. Go on home now, everyone. Lois is home."

Chapter Fifteen

"I scored a touchdown. "

June 5, 2016

It took a lot of strength to stay away from Sunset Place during the recommended adjustment period, but I talked to Jeanne every day on the phone, and she assured me everything was fine.

"Lois is a sweetheart," Jeanne said.

"Wait. Are you talking about my mother?" I asked, only half jokingly.

Jeanne said that Lois had already become a favorite with the staff.

"She is cheerful, and very appreciative of everything we do for her," she told me. "She seems to be enjoying her meals, and is joining in many of the activities."

"We can't be talking about the same woman," I said. "Mom always says she's not a 'joiner.'"

"Well, come at the end of the week, and see for yourself," Jeanne said. "Why don't you come for lunch? I'm sure Lois would enjoy that."

It was hard to wait until the end of the week, but, I hate to admit, I rather enjoyed having a few days off from overseeing Mom's care, and it was wonderful not having to monitor the nanny cam 24 hours a day, or to worry about her safety.

Nicole asked if she could stay in Mom's house, so I consulted Ed, Gary, and Pattie, who pointed out that the house needed to be occupied for insurance purposes and security.

"Once it gets around that nobody is living there, and it has furniture and all utilities, it'll be ransacked, looted, vandalized, or the copper pipes taken out," Pattie offered helpfully. "Kids will use it as a drug den or party place."

"Besides, Nicole stopped her month-to-month rental in Painesville, so if she doesn't stay at Mom's, she'll want to come back here with us," Gary said. "She drives us crazy, as I'm sure we do her, so that's not a good idea."

We decided to ask Nicole to pay for utilities while she was living there, but otherwise she could stay there rent free, at least until she found another job.

Nicole seemed relieved, and told me that was acceptable. She said she had already applied at several area nursing homes for caregiver jobs, but finding one that paid well, didn't require certification, and would accommodate her college schedule was harder to find than she thought.

That taken care of, at least for now, I made a list of items to get at Mom's and take to Sunset Place for

163

her, and another list of supplies she was going to need from Sam's Club. Adult diapers, wipes, hand soap, toothpaste, and maybe a few new fluffy towels. I made a mental note to check on whether she would need anything else when I would see her.

Late Friday morning, I drove the fifty minutes from my house to Sunset Place, anxious that all was going well, and hoping that Jeanne's daily reports on the phone had been truthful.

Lunch at the memory care wing of Sunset Place was served every day at noon. I arrived a little after eleven, thinking maybe I could help her get dressed.

I signed in at the front desk in the main lobby, and checked the guest book to see whether Mom had received any visitors this week. Nothing. At the door to the memory wing, I pushed the call button and waited until someone opened the door to buzz me in.

"Hold the door for me, please," said an older man on the other side of the door. "I need to get out."

"No you don't, Bill," an attendant, dressed in a colorful medical scrub, told him, taking him gently by the arm. "It'll be lunchtime soon, and you don't want to miss lunch, do you?"

Bill sighed, drooped his shoulders in resignation, and followed her.

Another uniformed attendant appeared. Her name tag read "GRACE." She was about 30 and wore her red hair in a practical pony tail. She asked who I was visiting.

"Lois," I told her. "She's my mom."

Grace's face lit up. "Oh, we all love Lois. She's so sweet. You'll find her in the exercise room straight down the hall. She's playing football."

Huh? My MOTHER?

"Wait," I said. "You must have another Lois here. My mother doesn't know one end of a football from another."

Grace smiled. "You'll be surprised. Go see. Do you think you can find it by yourself?"

I assured her I could, and headed down the hall to a room that seemed to be spilling laughter. I peeked into the room, and there was Mom, in her favorite sequined purple pant suit, kicking a brown egg-shaped balloon and giggling as others reached out to try taking it away from her.

Using her walker, she kicked the ball again and again, till she reached a plastic rectangular laundry basket, on its side, at one end of the room. With one mighty kick, Mom aimed the balloon right into the basket, dead center.

"I scored! I scored! Touchdown! Yay!" Mom declared, lifting her right hand, gripping the walker tightly with her left. I was as proud as a toddler's mom when her baby takes his first wobbly step.

"You cheated," accused an old man sporting a Korean War Veteran ballcap.

"No, she didn't, Bruce," a smiling attendant said. "You're just a little cranky this morning. You didn't have much breakfast. You'll feel better after lunch."

"No, I won't, with the crap you people serve," Bruce said. "I ate better in the Army mess hall."

Mom noticed me and her face lit up.

"Well, for cryin' out loud!" she exclaimed. "It's my daughter! Hi, Sweetie! I'm playing football! Can you believe it?"

I gave her a congratulatory hug.

"Now I have to go use the potty," she whispered.

"I'll take her," said Grace, who had just come into the room. "I'll get her washed and ready for lunch. We'll meet you in the dining room in a few minutes. There's a coffee pot always on there. Go help yourself."

"Come on, Lois," Grace said, taking Mom gently around one shoulder and steering her toward the door. "We'll get you ready for lunch, and a nice visit with your daughter."

"Okay," Mom said. "Where are we going?" she asked Grace, as the pair left the room.

I glanced around the half-empty exercise room. Most of the old people were seated in wheelchairs, demonstrating varying degrees of interest in what

166

was going on. One lady, dressed in a pink dress with pearls and a red feather boa around her neck, crooned lovingly to a baby doll she held on her lap. Another was rocking rhythmically back and forth, chanting wordlessly.

Bill appeared in the doorway.

"Say, could you let me out the main door?" he asked me. "I forgot my key and need to get home."

"Sorry, Bill, I can't," I told him. "I'm sure someone will be along soon to help you."

I made my way down the hall to the dining room and found the coffee pot, in a protected area that was hard to find or reach by most residents. I took a seat and glanced around the room. Two or three women sat in one corner, ignoring each other, their eyes focused intently on the door to the kitchen.

Gradually, people began to trickle in, with the help of canes, walkers, and wheel chairs. They ignored me as they headed to what appeared to be their accustomed seats. A few chatted with each other, but most of them just stared expectantly at the kitchen door.

More people appeared, this time with the help of an attendant, who would seat the person, tell them to stay put, and disappear to retrieve someone else.

Grace arrived, helping Mom keep steady with her walker.

"Well, for cryin' out loud!" Mom exclaimed as she approached the table where I was sitting. "How did you find me here at this restaurant?"

She sat down, clutching her purse tightly in her lap.

"They have good food here," she told me. "And reasonable prices. The service is pretty good too. Lunch is on me today, so order whatever you like. I don't care how much it is, even if it's more than $2. You're worth it."

An attendant came around with a coffee pot and a pitcher of apple juice. Each place already had glasses, coffee cups, and full, frosty glasses of water.

"If you'd like something besides apple juice, let me know," Grace said, as she poured Mom's coffee with one hand, and her apple juice in the other.

"Apple juice is fine, thanks," I told her.

"Lois's favorite is cranberry, but we're out of that today," Grace said.

Another attendant brought out two plates of food; on one plate was a hamburger-macaroni casserole with green beans; on the other was chicken salad on a bed of lettuce. Mom looked at both of them, trying to make up her mind.

"We give them two choices at each meal," the attendant explained. "It's less confusing for them that way. They also can order a la carte from the menu on the table, if they don't care for either

168

choice. They can always order soup and a sandwich if they prefer."

Mom indicated the macaroni casserole and I chose the chicken salad. It was excellent. Mom relished every bite of her casserole, and it dawned on me that it was the first dish Mom had taught me to cook, when I was nine. It remained one of my favorites.

"Here, have a bite," Mom said, proffering her loaded fork. "It's pretty good, but not as good as the one I taught you to make."

She was right.

Glancing around the dining room, I noticed that many of the residents picked at their food, or ignored it altogether. Some ate pureed food, and a few needed to be fed. The attendants gently encouraged everyone to eat. Once the main meal was consumed, the attendants removed the plates. Every eye, including both of Mom's, focused intently on the kitchen door.

"Dessert time!" Mom exclaimed, as the air got heavier with expectancy.

Within minutes, the door opened and an attendant wheeled a cart laden with desserts into the room. Thirty pairs of eyes strained with excitement, hoping to see the cart's contents.

"German chocolate cake! Hooray!" Mom exclaimed. "And if you don't want yours, I'll take it!"

She devoured her cake in a matter of seconds, then eyed mine. I pushed it over to her.

"Are you sure you don't want it?" Mom asked, pleased, as she attacked it.

Grace walked by.

"I can get you another piece if you like," she offered.

"Okay," I said. "Mom might want a third. Thanks."

After her third piece of cake, Mom wiped her mouth with her napkin, folded it, placed it on top of her plate, and announced, "Time to pay the bill and go home."

Uh oh.

"This is a very nice restaurant, but now I want to go home," she told me. "Please take me home. It's been fun, but I'm ready to go." She opened her purse.

"Lois, let me take care of that for you," Grace said. "I'll take you to the bathroom. Then would you like to watch the baseball game, or would you rather take a nap?"

"I need a nap," Mom said, walking away with Grace, who glanced back at me and said, "It's probably best for you to go now. She'll be fine once she's in bed. She's likely to sleep most of the afternoon."

Mom seemed unaware that I was even there, as she made her way, with Grace's help, down the hall to her room. She never once looked back. I walked over to the exit door and pushed the button to be buzzed out.

Bill appeared from nowhere.

"I'll go out with you," he said, smiling, with practiced nonchalance.

"No, Bill, you need to stay here," an attendant with a name tag reading "Sharonda" said as she buzzed the door open and took Bill by the hand. "The Indians game is on."

"What inning?" Bill asked her, as he walked away with her.

Chapter Sixteen

"I found a nice new restaurant."

September 12, 2016

Over the next few months, I fell into a pattern of visiting Mom every two to three days, usually at lunch. She always sat at one of the tables that faced the main door, her eyes focused intently on people going in and out, searching for a familiar face. It was as though she was meeting someone for lunch. As soon as she spotted me, her eyes lit up and she waved.

"YOO HOO! OVER HERE!" she called from across the room. None of the other residents appeared to notice.

"Well, for cryin' out loud!" Mom exclaimed as I approached. "How did you know I would be at this restaurant?"

She was wearing a light grey top printed with colorful birds, and pale blue slacks. A burgundy colored cloth napkin lay neatly on her lap, under her purse. I noticed that her fingernails were freshly polished, and Mom was grinning with delight.

I kissed her on the cheek and sat down at a vacant seat at her table. Two other ladies sat with her.

One, dressed in a yellow pants suit and pearls, frowned at me as I sat down.

"Who are you?" she groused.

"This is my daughter," Mom said brightly. "She has come to join me at lunch, although I have no idea how she knew I was here."

"One more mouth to feed," the woman complained. "I don't know how I'm going to manage. My paycheck will go only so far. They make me do all the work around here. I have to go in the back and iron all the napkins, and that's after I do all the cooking and wash all the dishes, not to mention the pots and pans. Nobody cares. Nobody."

She frowned at me intently.

"Give me my necklace," she commanded, reaching for the gold cross I was wearing. "That's mine. I've been looking for it for months. Give it here. Give. Gimme."

She frowned, crooked a finger at me, and reached closer. I pulled back, not quite knowing what to do.

"That's not yours, Pearl," an attendant, Sharonda, said as she brought two pitchers and began pouring water and juice. Pearl abruptly turned away from me, started crooning, "My Country 'Tis of Thee," and turned her attention to her apple juice.

"Do you want lunch?" Sharonda asked me. "Sorry about Pearl. She thinks she works here, and everything is hers. Keep an eye on your stuff when she's around. She's quick. Sunglasses, cell phones, wallets, pens, car keys. So lunch?"

"No thanks," I replied. "I'll get something on my way home. And thanks for the warning."

The other lady wore a sparkly pink top and an empty smile.

"Are you my daughter?" she asked.

Mom waved her off.

"No, she's my daughter. You get your own," she told her. "I saw her first."

"That's Ruby," Sharonda explained. "She's harmless. She and Pearl are sisters."

As I watched Mom devour her meatloaf, scalloped potatoes, and applesauce, I could see Bill hurrying down the hall where Mom's room was located. He peered behind him several times and tried to saunter casually, but the intent look on his face made me watch him with curiosity.

As he reached Mom's door, next to the locked outside entrance, he tried her doorknob, a hopeful look on his face. He sighed when he discovered it was locked. I could see him pondering his next move, glancing side to side, as he turned and headed for the outside door.

An alarm sounded, as every attendant dropped what they were doing and headed in that direction.

"I've got it," Grace yelled as she ran. "Bill again."

Grace hurried toward the door, calling, "No, Bill. Please stop." Bill saw her coming toward him, cried out in frustration, and threw his weight against the door, which didn't budge.

Grace gently took his arm and said, "You didn't finish your lunch, Bill. And we're having your favorite carrot cake for dessert. You don't want to miss that, do you? "

"All right," Bill said, as he followed Grace back to the dining room.

"What's all the commotion about?" Mom asked.

"Someone tried to leave without paying their bill," I lied.

"Shame on them," Mom said. "Honesty is the best policy."

"You're right," I agreed.

Mom opened her purse.

"I always pay my bills," she bragged. "So now we need to get the check so you can take me home."

"You ARE home," I ventured.

"What are you talking about?" Mom demanded. "Have you lost your mind? You know where my home is. Jakes Prairie, Missouri, with Mom, and Pop."

Her words took me aback. She hadn't lived in Missouri since 1930. Dad had built a house for her in Mentor in 1947, where she has lived ever since.

"Now, I'm a little tired," Mom told me. "Can you take me home now? I'd like to take a nap, in my own bed."

Sharonda appeared at that moment.

"Time for a nap, Lois," Sharonda told Mom. "Let me take you home. It's right down the hall."

Sharonda said I should probably go.

"See you later, Alligator," Mom called.

Chapter Seventeen

"At least I got pumpkin pie and M&Ms."

October 31, 2016

As I mentioned before, Mom was terrified of Halloween. This year, I worried about how she would handle it, if anyone in costume showed up at Sunset Place. I warned Grace and Sharonda that Mom might be frightened, and they thanked me for the warning.

When I arrived to sign in, I saw giant string spider webs, paper bats suspended on dental floss hanging here and there, and grinning jack-o-lanterns decorating the tables in the big dining hall and the hallway. The receptionist, Juan, was sporting a Zorro outfit, complete with mask.

I hope Mom doesn't see him, I thought. She would be scared to death. I carried a big Tupperware container of small M&Ms packs for everyone in the memory care unit as I buzzed to be let in.

Grace, sporting a Dorothy costume, complete with blue pinafore and red shoes, her long red hair in pigtails, opened the door for me.

"Is Mom okay?" I asked her, worried, as I passed through the door and into the dining room. I envisioned her barricaded in her room, trembling with fright.

Grace smiled. "I think you'll be pleasantly surprised," she assured me.

Mom sat at the usual table, and waved as she spotted me. She was wearing a cat ears headband and had thin black whiskers drawn to emanate from her pink lipsticked nose. A pink feather boa was wrapped jauntily around her neck. She was grinning from ear to ear.

"Look at me! I'm a cat! Meow!" she giggled. Across the table from Mom, Pearl was dressed as a princess, complete with tiara and wand, and Ruby wore Minnie Mouse ears (complete with bow) and a big red nose.

Mom hated cats, but she hated mice even more.

"Isn't this fun?" she asked. "And after lunch, they're bringing around some pre-school kids to trick or treat. I hope you brought some treats for me to give out. Especially M&Ms. They're my favorite I can't wait to see the kiddies in their costumes."

"Of course I brought treats," I told her, still reeling in disbelief as I opened the Tupperware. "But you can't have any unless you eat all of your lunch."

Familiar conversation from 60 years ago, but now in reverse. Life does that.

Mom scarfed down chicken noodle soup and a chicken salad sandwich, washed down with two glasses of cranberry juice.

"I really miss corn on the cob," she told me. "But it's never on the menu here at this restaurant. Do you think they'd get mad if you brought me some?"

"I'm sure that won't be a problem."

Why didn't I think of that before? Mom's favorite food in all the world was corn on the cob. She was, without a doubt, a lifelong corn connoisseur. At home, she would mark the calendar each mid August for the first day of corn season. She knew all the best corn stands in the county, and after I got my driver's license, she would send me to each of them to check out their corn. Her favorite was butter and cream, with its yellow and white kernels.

She taught me how to pick out the very best ears, by shape and plumpness. When I found the right one, I would carefully pull back the tasseled end and check for worms, which were usually at that end if they had invaded the cob.

She would inspect them with scientific expertise when I brought them home. If they weren't perfect, she would scowl and lecture me on what I had missed. If they were acceptable, my job would be to take them into the back yard and shuck them. I had better remove every last silk strand or I would hear about it.

Then they would go into the ancient, handle-less pot, full of boiling water, to which a spoonful of salt had been sprinkled. Mom would time it exactly for 10 minutes, no more and no less.

And, of course, corn on the cob wasn't complete without plenty of butter, salt, and a side of tomatoes.

I made a mental note to bring Mom some corn on the cob at every visit. And a salt shaker.

Mom, Ruby, Pearl, and all the other residents focused on the door to the kitchen, eager for dessert. The anticipation bubbled up until it was almost tangible, as all (who could) sat up straight, conversation ceased, dolls were put aside, and all waited for the high point of their day.

Finally, the door opened, and Sharonda pushed the dessert cart into the room. Everyone began buzzing: PUMPKIN PIE! With Whipped Cream! Oh, it was a very good day indeed!

Sharonda offered me a piece after all the residents had received theirs.

"Happy Halloween," she whispered. "No charge."

By the time I thanked her, Mom had already finished her piece and was eyeing mine. I pushed it over to her, and she dug in with the eagerness of a child.

After the dishes were cleared, I grabbed a cup of coffee, as the residents were each given a small pile of wrapped candy.

"Don't you be eating more than a piece," Grace cautioned everyone. "We don't want you getting sick. In a few minutes, the kids from Miss Alicia's Pre School will be coming in to trick or treat. You can give them candy when they hold out their pumpkins."

The anticipation rose again.

"I have to go to the bathroom," announced Pearl. "Uh oh. Too late."

An attendant came and wheeled Pearl back to her room for a change.

"Can I have her candy?" Ruby asked.

Mom reached over and grabbed some packs of M&Ms from Pearl's pile.

"She won't mind," Mom said. "They're my favorite. Finders keepers, losers weepers."

I opened the Tupperware and added several more packs of M&Ms to both of their piles and made a small pile for myself, as the big door opened and Miss Alicia, accompanied by several proud parents sporting cameras, walked in among a stream of two dozen little ones.

There were lions, and firefighters, and Spidermen, and Mickey Mice, and many, many Elsas and Annas from the current Disney hit, "Frozen." I recognized them because my granddaughters were obsessed with Elsa and Anna, always arguing whose turn it was to be the more glamorous Elsa.

"Aren't they cute?" Mom asked, as she held out a Reese's candy bar to a miniature Batman.

"Here you go, Honey," she said. "Are you my grandson?"

"No, Mom, your grandkids are all grown up, but you have three great-granddaughters and one great-grandson, so far."

"I do? Do I know them?"

"Yes, you've seen them many times. There's Bridget, Clare, Norah, and little Jack," I told her.

"Jack? After my Jack? How wonderful!" Mom exclaimed, for probably the 600th time. "Whose is he?"

"Katie's little boy. They live in South Carolina," I told her, for the 600th time.

"South Carolina! Near the ocean?" she asked.

"No, they live in the Upstate, in the mountains," I told her.

"Well, can they see the ocean from where they are?" she asked.

"No, they're about four hours away."

"Named for my Jack," she said in wonder. "We'll have to do something special for him in my will."

One positive thing about Alzheimer's is, I got to deliver good news to her, like the birth of a great-grandchild, over and over again, and Mom got to celebrate it many, many times.

We gave away most of the remaining candy, as the little ones finished their rounds, thanked us, waved goodbye, and trooped out, their pumpkins full. Mom opened another little pack of M&Ms, put it to her mouth, and slid the candies in.

"I think I'm tired now," she said. "I want to pay the bill and go home."

"I'm glad you enjoyed Halloween," I told her.

"I did?" Mom asked, incredulous. "It's Halloween? I hate Halloween! I need to go to bed, now!" A look of sheer panic took over her face.

Sharonda helped her stand up, placed her walker within reach, and helped her totter down the hall to her room.

Mom didn't even say goodbye.

Chapter Eighteen

"Happy Birthday to somebody."

November 23, 2016

Mom's 97th birthday was a very big deal. First, we didn't know whether it would be her last, and second, the whole family was in town to celebrate Thanksgiving together: Gary, Pattie, their three girls Nicole, Kelly, and Jessie, our daughters Megan and Katie, their spouses Matt and David, Megan's girls Bridget, Clare, and baby Norah, and Katie's boy, little Jack, both toddlers.

Pattie brought Kentucky Fried Chicken and all the side dishes, I brought a dozen ears of corn, a big sheet cake, and ice cream, and the granddaughters brought decorations, including two huge balloons--- one a 9 and the other a 7, balloons for the little kids, flowers, and a plastic tiara with I'M 97! on it in big pink letters.

When all was ready, Gary walked down to Mom's room and wheeled her to the party.

"Surprise!" we all yelled.

"Well, for cryin' out loud!" Mom exclaimed. "Is it somebody's birthday or something?"

"It's yours, Great Grandma!" Clare said.

"How old am I?" Mom asked, staring at the balloons.

"How old do you think, Mom?" I asked her.

"Well, I feel close to a hundred," she replied.

"That's close," I said. "97."

"I knew I was born in 1919, but I can't recall what year it is now," she said. "How did you find me at this restaurant?"

"You're always here," I told her.

Mom rolled her eyes.

"You exaggerate," she pouted. "I've only eaten here once or twice. It's pretty good."

Mom tore into the corn on the cob first, devouring three cobs before we reminded her that there was also chicken. She ate a drumstick, mashed potatoes and gravy, green beans, and a biscuit, then asked for dessert.

After everyone, including Mom, sang an enthusiastic rendition of Happy Birthday, the French doors opened, and two ladies, with walkers, joined us.

"Have some cake," Mom offered. "It's somebody's birthday. I made it."

The ladies each took a paper plate with cake and ice cream.

"It was nice of you to join us," I told them, after they introduced themselves as Irene and Eloise.

"How do you know Mom?" I asked them.

"Oh, we don't know her from Adam," Irene said. "We just saw through the glass on the doors that you were serving cake."

Lucky for us, it was a big cake.

When it was time for presents, Mom said, "I don't think I brought one. Whose birthday is it?"

"Yours, Mom," I said. "So open your gifts."

New slippers, a robe, three boxes of candy, a tin of home-made cookies, and a vase of her favorite roses.

"How nice!" Mom exclaimed. "I'm tired now. I want to go home and go to bed."

Everyone pitched in to clean up. Ed carried the remainder of the cake to the attendants' break room, where someone placed it on their table, thanked us, and promised to save pieces for Grace and Sharonda.

The girls brought the gifts and decorations, as I wheeled Mom to her room. Her door was unlocked again, which was not supposed to be the case. I made a mental note to take that up with Nancy, the head nurse, next time I saw her.

We bundled Mom into bed, under her photo blanket.

"This was a very nice day," she said. "Thank you all for coming. Whoever's birthday it was, Happy Birthday."

Chapter Nineteen

I baked my famous Christmas cookies.

December 20, 2016

I ran a little late getting to Sunset Place one day shortly before Christmas. Lunch was already over, and most of the residents were dozing around the TV. The room was bedecked in red and green paper chains similar to the ones my fourth graders had made for our classroom every year. In front of the window was a Christmas tree twinkling with white lights.

I glanced around the room for Mom, who was nowhere to be seen. I walked down to her room and found the door unlocked, so I peeked in. No Mom.

"Yoo hoo!" I called as I walked in. No one in the chair or the bed, and the bathroom was empty. Hmmm.

Back in the living room, I spotted Sharonda, who was wheeling a sleeping Ruby away to her room. I asked her where Mom was hiding.

"You won't believe this, but she's at choir practice in the main assisted living section," she informed me.

"Go on!" I said.

"No, really," she said, grinning. "We asked if anyone wanted to sing Christmas carols at our holiday party on Christmas Eve, and Lois raised her hand. Your mother has a beautiful singing voice."

"She always loved to sing, especially hymns and Christmas carols," I told her.

Sharonda told me I could find her in the main dining room in the assisted living section. Sure enough, seated in the back of the room, Mom was concentrating on a music book as an attendant tried to lead about 12 people in "Away in a Manger."

Not wanting Mom to spot me and start waving and yelling, I watched from a distance. Mom strained to look at the page, frowned, closed the book, and set it in her lap. She used to teach us all verses of just about every Christmas carol ever written, even the ones in German.

As the leader began the second verse, Mom belted it out, only slightly off key. She didn't hesitate on any of the words, but she was the only one singing.

"Thank you, Lois," the attendant said. "But it looks like we'll be doing only one verse. Maybe more than one is too much."

"People are lazy," Mom observed.

I noticed that Mom was sitting in a wheel chair. It was probably a lot easier, and quicker, to transport her from one wing to the other. I made a mental note to ask Nancy, the RN in charge of the memory care wing, about the change, and whether it was temporary or permanent.

Mom was excited to see me.

"There's my daughter!" she yelled, waving with enthusiasm. "Well, for cryin' out loud!

"How did you know where to find me?" she asked when I reached her and kissed her hello on the cheek.

"I'm psychic," I told her.

"No, you're not," she said. "Have you come to take me home?"

The attendant announced that practice was over, so I wheeled Mom back to the memory care wing and buzzed for entrance.

Grace opened the door, as Bill, lurking behind her, decided to make a run for it. Mom's wheelchair blocked the door, which slowed his escape.

"No, you don't, Bill," Grace said, gently taking his arm. Resigned at being caught once again, Bill shrugged, made an about face, and followed her back into the unit, as I wheeled Mom in and proceeded down the hall to her room.

"I have to go potty," Mom whispered.

I wheeled her to her bathroom door, and, using the bars on the walls, she managed to swing herself into the room, use the toilet, and wash her hands. She leaned on me as I walked her to the bed, removed her shoes, and helped her under the covers.

"I made Christmas cookies," she bragged. "All of your favorites. Get one for yourself in one of the tins on the back porch before you go, but only take one. Dad needs to take some to the office. I'm a little tired, and I think I'll take a nap until your dad gets home from work."

I sat with her until she was snoring. When she was deeply asleep, she started murmuring something. I strained to hear.

"The cattle are lowing, the poor Baby wakes," she sang. "But little Lord Jesus, no crying he makes..."

Noticing that my face was leaking again, I wiped away the moisture, kissed her on the forehead, and tiptoed out.

Sharonda asked if Mom was asleep. I told her yes.

"Did she tell you we made Christmas cookies this morning?" she asked me. "We made them for the holiday party, but I don't recommend anyone eating any of them except Lois's."

"Why is that?"

Sharonda smiled.

"Most of the residents would put the knife in the can of frosting and lick the knife before spreading the frosting on the cookies," she said, chuckling. "But not Lois. Was she a professional baker by any chance?"

"Almost," I replied. "She took lessons in cake decorating fifty years ago, before fancy cakes became competitions, and she was famous for her

190

character cakes and doll cakes. She was always a talented and meticulous baker."

"Well, I watched the residents as we decorated the cookies. Lois's were perfect, and she never once licked the knife."

Proud daughter moment.

The afternoon before Christmas Eve, the family all swooped into Sunset Place for the Christmas concert and party. Rows of seats had been placed in the secondary dining room, with some also in the adjoining living room, as the aroma of freshly popped popcorn filled the air.

Gary and Pattie, their girls, Ed and I, with our older daughter Megan and her family, which included our three granddaughters, took up one whole row of chairs. The little girls all wore their Christmas dresses, tights, and dress shoes, with their hair in neat pony tails held back with red ribbons.

Soon after we settled into our seats, residents filed into a row facing the audience. Most were in wheelchairs. Mom was wheeled into a spot close to us, and she waved as she spotted us.

"Yoo hoo!" Mom yelled. She was dressed in green slacks and a red sweatshirt covered in brown reindeer. The antlers sported tiny bells that tinkled every time she moved. The shirt proclaimed "GRANDMA'S LITTLE DEERS," and each reindeer bore the name of one of her four great-grandchildren. I had ordered it for her from a catalog because all of her previous holiday outfits were way too big on her now and had been donated to charity during our purge.

Then I noticed that one of the attendants had placed reindeer antlers on a plastic headband on Mom's head. She seemed oblivious to it.

The "choir" consisted of six residents, who sang the first verses of three Christmas songs: Away in a Manger, Rudolph the Red Nosed Reindeer, and We Wish You a Merry Christmas. Mom grinned silently at us the whole time, completely forgetting to sing.

We clapped with enthusiasm anyway, just as we had for our girls' pre-school concerts so many years ago.

After the concert, we sat around a big table in the dining room, with Mom at the head. One by one, each grandchild or great-grandchild went up to her, gave her a hug, and told her their name.

Mom apologized for not having any presents for anyone.

"It's so hard to shop for everyone," she sighed. "And I don't know anyone's sizes. Well, Merry Christmas, anyway."

Each great-grandchild proudly presented her with a crayoned "selfie" self-portrait, each one signed with their carefully written name. Norah's drawings was a one-color scrawl in green.

Attendants brought around cups of punch and plates of cookies.

"We had to use store-bought for safety's sake," Grace whispered to me. "But I put some of your mom's cookies on the plate for the grandkids. Lois's are safe to eat."

After refreshments, Mom declared she was ready to go home for a nap.

"Thank you all for coming to see an old lady," she said. "Merry Christmas to all of you. You're all so nice to come for a visit. I wish I knew your names."

As Grace wheeled Mom away, we could hear her crooning, "Rudoph, the Red Nosed Reindeer."

Chapter Twenty

March 21, 2017

"Did you remember the salt?"

Shortly after New Year's, I began to see the steady decline escalating in Mom. She was in the wheelchair all the time now, and was losing weight. But every time I entered the unit, she would yell a hearty "Yoo Hoo!" from across the room and wave like a cheerleader. Her eyesight was still razor sharp, and she still recognized me.

"Well, for cryin' out loud!" she'd exclaim, taking my hand as I kissed her on the cheek. "How did you find me at this restaurant?"

"Hi, Mom. You eat here every day," would be my daily reply.

"Nah, you're exaggerating," she'd said. "I've only been here a few times."

"Mom, you live here," I'd say gently.

"Don't lie to me, young lady," she'd snort. "You know very well that I live on the Prairie. I just decided to come here for lunch."

She would turn to Ruby and Pearl.

"This is my daughter, Diane," she would say proudly.

"I know," groused Pearl. "You're my boss, always making me do more work all the time. Working me to the bone, and what thanks do I get?"

"How do you do?" said Ruby politely, looking down at the napkin on her lap.

Mom would then whisper to me behind her hand.

"I have no idea who they are, but they are very nice, whatever their names are," she would tell me. "For some reason, they wanted to sit with me. Is that okay?"

"Of course, Mom, the more, the merrier," I'd say.

But on this blustery March day, Ruby and Pearl were missing. Mom and I sat alone at the table. I glanced around to see where they went, but they weren't anywhere in the room.

"Where are the sisters?" I asked Grace, who was serving the soup.

"They are in their room," she answered. "They both have the flu, and we're keeping them isolated from the other residents."

I looked at Mom, who was stirring her soup and frowning at it, glancing around the table for a salt shaker. She looked fine, at least so far.

"Got any salt?" she asked. "The food is good here, but it needs a little salt, and they don't put a salt shaker on the table."

"I'll bring you a salt shaker next time I come," I promised.

I watched her closely as she ate, looking for signs of nausea or fever. She grinned at me as I put my hand on her forehead. No fever.

"Have a bite of this Swiss steak," she said, proffering her fork. "It's pretty good, but it could use a little more salt."

I repeated my promise to bring her a salt shaker on my next visit.

After lunch, I wheeled her down to her room. As I opened the door, I noticed a tall male figure disappearing into Mom's closet. My normal reaction would have been to wheel her back out into the hall and call for help, but I recognized the ball cap. Mom sucked in her breath, alarmed but too surprised to say anything.

"Hi, Bill," I called. "You're in the wrong room."

Bill poked his head out of the closet door.

"I was trying to find the door to go out," Bill said. "Maybe you could help me. I need to leave."

Poor guy.

"Sure, Bill. Follow me," I said, taking his hand and leading him into the hall. I spotted Sharonda coming out of one of the other rooms on the corridor and called to her.

"Bill! I was just looking for you!" Sharonda said, taking his hand. He meekly followed her back down the hall.

As I got Mom ready for her afternoon nap, it bothered me that Bill was finding his way into Mom's room, that was supposed to be kept locked from the hallway. He seemed harmless enough, but Mom was completely vulnerable, especially when she was in bed. I hated to think about anyone trying to hurt her, but the poor, confused people in this unit might mistake her for their spouse or something. I needed to have a talk with Head Nurse Nancy as soon as possible. I know it's inconvenient to hunt down someone with a key every time I needed to go into Mom's room, but she needed to be safe.

Once Mom was asleep, I hunted down Nancy, who was dispensing medications in the nurses' room.

"I found Bill in Mom's room just now," I told her. "He was hiding in her closet. He said he was trying to find the door out."

Nancy set down a bottle of pills and sighed. "Not again," she said.

"How often do you find him in Mom's room?"

"Every few days," Nancy answered. "The door is supposed to be kept locked, but sometimes the aides are too busy to remember. I'll make sure it doesn't happen again. Bill is harmless, but he shouldn't be hiding in Lois's room."

"Mom is completely vulnerable, and she needs to be kept safe at all times," I reminded her. She promised to talk to the attendants.

Next morning, before I could leave for Sunset Place, my cell phone rang. The caller ID indicated it was Nancy.

She explained to me that the entire wing was on quarantine, after six more residents came down with the flu overnight, including Bill. She assured me that Mom was fine so far. Everyone was confined to their rooms, and their food brought to them. Attendants were checking them every half hour.

"How is she taking it?" I asked Nancy. "Can I see her?"

"Not unless you are a staff member dressed in a surgical gown and mask," she said. "We have a regular protocol for breakouts of contagious diseases. We will probably be shut down for several days, maybe a week, until no one has any more symptoms. Don't worry. Lois is fine. No symptoms so far. Right now she's in her recliner watching an old Cary Grant movie on her TV. She had a big breakfast and is in good spirits. We are monitoring her closely."

Nancy promised to call with updates every day, and gave me the direct phone number for the public information officer, who would be available 24/7 to answer any questions.

I called Gary and Nicole and informed them about the latest developments. The quarantine lasted nine days altogether. When I got the word that there were no more flu symptoms among the residents and staff, and that the entire facility had been disinfected twice before being open again to visitors, I headed for Sunset Place, armed with Mom's favorite corn on the cob, cooked and stuffed into a Ziploc bag.

"Well, for cryin' out loud!" Mom exclaimed as she spotted me. "Where've you been?"

I explained that no visitors had been allowed for several days because of a flu outbreak.

"I'm not sick," Mom announced. "Did I get a flu shot this year?"

I told her that she had, and showed her the surprise I had with me.

"You brought me corn!" Mom cried in delight. "Did you bring butter, salt, and corn holders?"

I pulled them all out of another Ziploc. I put the holders on either end of a cob, still warm from sitting in my car window on the trip in. Mom's smile lit up the room as she sprinkled salt on the slightly buttered corn.

"Where did you get the salt?" she whispered. "They always forget to put it on the table. This shaker looks familiar."

"It's yours. From your house," I assured her.

Like a Bugs Bunny cartoon, Mom buzzed back and forth on the ear of corn as if it was a row of typing and she was in a speed contest. She quickly finished it and eyed the other one in the bag. I prepared it for her, and watched contentedly as she salted that one and started eating.

"This sure is good," she beamed. "It's been a long time."

From then on, I became known as Corn Lady during my visits to Sunset Place. Each visit, I brought Mom two cobs of corn, enjoying the look of pure joy on her face.

Pearl, now recovered from the flu, complained that Mom was leaving a mess as she ate it.

"Who's going to clean that up?" Pearl groused. "Not me. I'm on vacation."

Mom dutifully picked up the spilled kernels from the table, and before I could stop her, popped them in her mouth.

"This is so good," she purred. "I don't want to miss one little bit of it."

She reached into her pocket and pulled out a rumpled Kleenex to wipe her mouth, ignoring the cloth napkin neatly folded in her lap. With the Kleenex came three empty plastic containers of coffee creamer and four chewed up sugar packets.

As Grace walked by, I pointed out the purloined items in Mom's hand.

"Oh, yes, Lois is a thief," she chuckled. "We had to stop putting the creamers and sugar packets on the tables, because many residents were putting them in their pockets and making a real mess. Lois must have kept those hidden pretty well." She scooped them up to throw them away.

"What about salt shakers?" I asked. "Mom is used to salting everything, and she keeps asking for it."

Grace smiled again.

"I'll bring one and you can see for yourself," she told me.

When Grace brought the glass salt shaker, Mom grabbed it immediately like a greedy child. As I watched in horror, Mom unscrewed the shaker top, raised the glass base to her lips, and proceeded to pour the salt into her mouth.

"No, Mom, please don't eat the salt," I chided her gently, as I took the shaker from her hand.

Mom frowned.

"I just wanted a little taste," she pouted.

I told Grace I understood. She suggested I bring a small salt shaker each visit, let Mom sprinkle salt on her food, then take the shaker back home with me.

Each time, Mom would whisper as I out the shaker back in my bag, "Are you stealing it? Won't you get in trouble? Maybe I should pay them for it," reaching for her purse.

"No, Mom, it's okay. This is mine from home."

This ritual continued throughout the summer and fall. Each time, Mom would be surprised at the treat. By Thanksgiving, she went from two cobs to one, and by Christmas, she would take only a few bites.

By Valentine's Day, she didn't recognize what it was and told me she wasn't hungry.

Chapter Twenty-one

I still have my marbles; I've just forgotten where I put them.

February 14, 2018

As winter continued to slam the lakeshore area of northeast Ohio, Mom was oblivious to the weather or the time of year. She seemed content to be cleaned up and dressed every morning, wheeled down to the dining room for breakfast, wheeled back to her room for a nap, wheeled back to the dining room for lunch, wheeled to the living room for socialization (which usually resulted in a nap), wheeled to the dining room for an evening snack, and wheeled back to her room to prepare for the night.

She never asked about going home anymore. She also seemed unaware of the others at her table, and didn't question when Pearl and Ruby were no longer at the table, transferred to another facility.

"Your mom is a sweetheart," Grace told me one afternoon. "She is always so grateful for every little thing we do for her, and she never complains about anything. Except when we give her a shower once a week. Then she fights us like a tiger."

"She never took showers, only baths at home," I told her. "There was only one tub in the house, and no working shower head. As she got older, we put a seat in the bathtub, but even that got too hard for her.

Home health aides helped her, but a bath became an ordeal, and after she was restricted to the first floor, most of the time she would just wash in the downstairs powder room sink twice a day."

I suggested that Sunset Place install a walk-in tub for the residents to take a good, soaking tub bath from time to time.

"That's a great idea," Grace said, her red pony tail bobbing as she nodded. "I'll pass that along, but it would probably get more attention if it came from you."

For Valentine's Day, Sunset Place served a special lunch---a choice of heart-shaped meatloaf or chicken tenders, mashed potatoes, green beans, red jello, and red velvet cake. Mom ate a few bites of mashed potatoes, half the jello, and every bite of the cake. I rewarded her with a pack of M&Ms, which I slipped to her two at a time, pretending it was contraband. Mom giggled.

"What happens if we get caught?" she asked, munching them two at a time.

"They will eat them instead of us," I replied with a wink.

After lunch, I wheeled her into the auxiliary dining room, which was used for those who needed to be fed, as well as an activity room for coloring and group activities, and for meal visits with family. We had used it several times when the grandkids were visiting, and Mom always loved to watch them coloring, even if she had no idea who they were.

After she was settled in her wheelchair at a small table, I set a package in front of her that was wrapped in paper decked with pink and red hearts.

"Happy Valentine's Day, Mom," I said.

"What's this?" she asked, her eyes wide with anticipation as she struggled to tear open the paper. I thought back to all the times we had to open the paper very carefully so she could save it to wrap another gift. Most wrapping paper in our house usually went through three or four cycles.

She recognized the book's cover immediately. LOIS: A CENTURY IN PICTURES.

"Oh, my," she said. "That's my baby picture. How did it get onto a book?"

I explained that I had a book made of photos from her life, beginning as a baby almost one hundred years ago.

She turned each page slowly, exclaiming as photo after photo told the story of her life.

"There's me with my sisters Amy and Opal, and brothers Russell, Buell, and Marty," she said without hesitation. "I was two. It was taken in front of our house on Jakes Prairie. Uncle Sam Jackson had a camera, and one Sunday Mom lined us up for a photo."

One by one, she recognized herself with her mom and dad, standing in front of their Model T, her dad driving a hay wagon drawn by a pair of mules, her mom feeding the flock of chickens, her school pictures, photos with her friends on the beach, in a prom gown, in her high school cap and gown, and with Dad.

"How on earth were you able to do this?" she marveled, continuing to turn the pages slowly.

She recognized her wedding photo, pictures of dad and her building their house, and my baby pictures.

"You were a cute baby, but you had your days and nights mixed," she told me. "I thought I never was going to get a good night's sleep ever again."

She paused at a family Christmas picture from 1956.

"Oh, my," she said, her voice cracking as a tear rolled down her cheek. "There we were, all of us. Ken was still alive. I miss him so much. And Jack. The love of my life."

I could only nod, amazed that she recognized everyone. I hadn't seen her mind this clear in four or five years. I blew my nose, surprised to discover that my face was leaking.

She looked up from the book, wiped away a tear from my cheek with her ever-present Kleenex, and patted my hand.

"Honey, this is the best present you could ever have given me. I love seeing everyone again," Mom said.

She turned the pages a little faster as she saw the more recent photos, of our spouses, children, and grandchildren.

206

"These people all look familiar; do they belong to me too?" she asked. I went over the labeled photos, one by one, and identified each face. A younger, smiling image of herself was in many of the photos---rocking one of the babies, baking a birthday cake for Katie's fifth birthday, posing with Megan in her high school cap and gown, with Gary's family, the surprise party we gave in Florida for Mom and Dad on their fiftieth anniversary in 1996, our 1997 road trip---Dad, Mom, and I---from Columbus to Tucson to Lake Tahoe, working jigsaw puzzles with her smiling great-grandchildren ; her life history in front of her eyes.

She closed the book, sighed, and looked at me intently.

"I want to know, why am I here?" she asked me, point blank. "I mean, they treat me wonderful here, but I know this is not home. So why am I here?"

I explained to her, as gently as I could, that she had fallen at home and had been in the hospital, then a rehab center, for several weeks.

"The doctor determined that it wasn't safe for you to be at home by yourself anymore," I said. "Gary and I tried to keep you in the house as long as we could, but it just wasn't safe for you there anymore. So we did some research and found this place, with a beautiful room that could accommodate your bed. We thought it's what Dad would have wanted." I scanned her face for a response.

After a few moments of reflection, she quietly nodded, then reached over and patted my hand.

"You did the right thing," she whispered.

I looked up at the ceiling, tears flowing in earnest now, thanked God for Mom's rare moment of clarity, and ended with a soft whisper, "Thanks, Dad."

Chapter Twenty-two

"Who's that strange man in my room?"

May 11, 2018

As the year progressed, so did Mom's dementia. She became more and more frail, and more susceptible to falls. About every other week, I received calls, usually from Head Nurse Nancy, that would be variations on the following:

"Diane? It's Nancy. Everything is okay, so don't worry, but your Mom had another fall during the night. She apparently tried to get up to go to the bathroom after we did our hourly check, and she slid off the edge of her bed and onto the floor. She wasn't hurt, but she couldn't get up, so she was on the floor until we did our next bed check. She wasn't in any distress. As a matter of fact, she was sound asleep on the floor and had pulled the comforter and pillow down to be more comfortable and cover herself up."

"Thanks for telling me, Nancy. She's okay then? No bumps or bruises?"

"She's fine. She just had her breakfast, and she didn't remember falling at all."

"Good thing her bed is so low to the floor, I guess," I said. "Not very far to fall."

"Now about the bed," Nancy said. "Would you consider putting her into a hospital bed instead of the king? It's a lot of work to change it, which we have to do pretty frequently now."

"No. I think you know the answer," I said. "Except for the time at home that we had to restrict her to the first floor, she has slept in that bed for 50 years. It represents home, and security, to her. It took the place of the farm homestead her family lost in Missouri when Mom was a child. We selected that room specifically so she could sleep in her own bed. It means everything to her."

Nancy sighed. "Well, I thought it was worth a try. The staff has been grumbling that it's a lot of work."

"That's what we're paying for," I replied. "No, that bed stays. We had her in a hospital bed for a few months at home, and she was miserable. She couldn't sleep, and kept wandering the house at night. The bed is non-negotiable. Sorry."

I arrived at Sunset Place mid morning so I could make sure she was okay before wheeling her down to lunch. Nancy gave me a key to Mom's door, but when I tried the knob before inserting the key, it turned easily. Unlocked. Not good. But maybe the staff was in there with her.

When I tried to push the door open, it was blocked from inside. I pushed hard, and the barricade moved slightly, just enough for me to squeeze inside.

There, inside the room, near the doorway, in the darkness, sat a large, hulking man in a wheelchair.

210

Holding my alarm in check, I scanned the room, and there was Mom in her bed, struggling to sit up, a startled, terrified look on her face.

"YOO HOO!" she yelled, waving frantically, as she recognized me.

Relieved that, number one, Mom appeared to be okay, although shaken, and more important, number 2, that the man was nowhere near her, I asked him what he was doing.

"I'm the security guard," he answered in an authoritative voice. "I've been assigned to guard this room."

Uh huh.

I backed out the door, grabbing the handles of his wheelchair and pulling it firmly but calmly, backwards toward the hall.

"Thank you for your help," I said, not missing a beat. "I'm here now to relieve you. Your shift is over."

Just then, frantic attendants ran toward us.

"Roscoe! There you are! We've been searching all over for you!" they yelled.

I glared at them as they wheeled him away.

"This is what happens when you FORGET TO LOCK THE DOORS!" I yelled. Normally I'm not a yeller by nature, but Mom could have been hurt. She was completely vulnerable, a tiny figure in a huge bed, and, although good old Roscoe seemed harmless enough, it could easily have been someone who thought Mom was his wife, if you get my meaning.

Needless to say, as soon as I calmed down and got Mom situated, I was going to have a nice little impromptu visit with the Sunset Place CEO.

Mom was cheerful when I went back to her room, and had no memory of what had just occurred.

"Well, for cryin' out loud!" she exclaimed as walked in her door. "How did you find me?"

"Mom, you live here," I said, searching her face for signs of distress and her visible skin for any signs of abuse.

"No, I don't! You exaggerate!" she said. "Is it time for lunch yet? I thought we'd try this new restaurant right down the street. What do you say? I hear that the food is good and the prices are not too high. I'll even treat."

After lunch, I turned her over to Sharonda and headed to the CEO's office, expecting to see Steve, the head honcho. But the sign on the open door read LaMonique Robinson, CEO. Wonder what happened to Steve. He'd been there only a few months.

"Can I help you?" an attractive woman in her mid 40s asked pleasantly, as she waved me into her office and indicated a seat opposite her desk.

I explained the morning incident to her, and she listened intently, writing down a few notes during the discussion.

"I totally agree with you; this is unacceptable," she told me. "I can imagine your concern when you found the man in your mother's room. All I can tell you is, we've had a lot of turnover in personnel lately, which is very common in our industry, and it sounds like someone dropped the ball in either training new people or in laxity of following procedure."

"I'm grateful that nothing apparently happened, but it could have," I told her. "If I hadn't been there, there's no telling what could have happened to my mother. And who knows how long it would have taken the staff to work their way all the way down the hall to Mom's room when they searched for Roscoe? This could have been a tragedy."

"I totally agree," she said again.

"That's all well and good, but what can you do to prevent this from happening again? That door must be kept locked, and Mom can't do it herself. She used to, but she's way beyond that capability now. So how can we keep her safe, short of me sitting with her 24/7?"

LaMonique thought about that. Steve wouldn't have hesitated. But under Steve's leadership, it probably wouldn't have happened in the first place.

No. That wasn't fair. Steve had dropped the ball a few times himself.

"I will meet with staff in their break room after the residents' lunch," LaMonique said. "This is totally unacceptable, and I can guarantee you, it will not happen again. Your mother's room will be kept locked from the outside at all times, whether or not she is in the room."

I told her about Bill's strategy of using Mom's room as part of his escape plan.

"Yes, I know all about Bill," she said with a wry smile. "We are working hard to keep him from trying to leave, and I promise he will not be able to use your mom's room as his escape hatch anymore."

Unconvinced but willing to give LaMonique the benefit of the doubt, I wished her success, and left to run a few errands on the way home. I needed to close out Mom's safe deposit box at the bank branch closest to her house. We hadn't used the box in a few months, but I had kept the keys to it, just in case we needed it for some reason. Recently I had decided that we really didn't need it anymore, and I was more than a little afraid of losing one or both of the keys, so I decided to turn them in and discontinue having the box altogether.

The bank teller suggested that I check the box one more time before turning over the keys, just in case I had inadvertently left something in it. Although I was sure I hadn't, it didn't hurt to be thorough.

After I confirmed it was, indeed, completely empty, I turned in the keys, ending another small chapter in Mom's life. She and Dad had had that box since the 1970s, right after their break-in. Dad had made a series of slides, photographic evidence of all their valuables, and had stored a few small heirlooms that the thieves had missed.

I was remembering that break-in, from so long ago, as I walked toward the door, probably for the last time.

A familiar voice called my name in surprise, but the surprise was mine when I looked to see who it was.

Her red hair was in a sleek new style, and the ponytail was gone, but the smiling bank teller looked very familiar. I couldn't quite place her.

"Diane? How's your mom?"

Aha!

"Grace! Wow! What are you doing here? I hadn't seen you at Sunset Place for a few days, but I just thought you were on vacation."

Grace shook her head.

"I couldn't handle it there anymore, so I took a job here last week," Grace explained. "I loved the residents, especially Lois, but the pressure and company demands just got to be too much for the size of the paycheck. I make better money here, the hours are better, and no more hassles."

I told her I was happy for her but sad for Mom.

"You were wonderful with her," I told Grace. "She is going to miss you."

Grace smiled. "Maybe for a few minutes, but I bet she has already forgotten me. That's how dementia is."

So true.

I wished Grace well, and went on my way.

Chapter Twenty-three

"What's that staple in my head?"

July 16, 2018

My cell rang very early, a clue that it was someone from Sunset Place, and it wasn't good news. Caller ID confirmed my suspicion.

"Good morning," said Nancy. "Your mom had a nasty fall a few minutes ago when we were with her in the bathroom. She lost her balance and hit her head on the towel bar as she went down. The attendant tried to catch her, but it happened very fast."

"Is she okay?" I asked, fighting down the rising panic.

"She's awake, but she has a nasty cut on her head and a few bruises. She's alert and doesn't seem to be in any pain. The ambulance is on its way. You can meet her at Lake West's emergency room by the time you can drive here. Do you know how to get there?"

"We're kind of frequent flyers there," I assured her. "Tell Mom I'm on my way."

As Ed drove, I called Gary, Nicole, and our two girls. I hesitated getting them all worried, since there was nothing they could do from so far away, but Ed, who is usually right, said they would want to be in the loop. I figured Gary would be in charge of telling his other two girls, although knowing Nicole, she had probably tweeted her sisters already.

Lake West Hospital is almost an hour from our house, no matter what shortcut we try. By the time we found Mom's room in the emergency department, it was already crowded with my brother's entire family. Mom was wearing a hospital gown and was propped up in bed, grinning with all the attention, as Nicole helped her drink some water from a straw in a plastic cup.

"Well, for cryin' out loud," Mom exclaimed when she saw me. "How did you know I was here?"

"I always know where you are, Mom," I said, kissing her on the cheek. "How are you feeling?"

"I'm happy to see everyone," she said. "I don't know how I got here, but everybody here is very nice."

A nurse entered the room and said they had already administered several tests, starting with a CAT scan, and no bones were broken, and no sign of any serious injury.

"She has quite a gash on the back of her head, and we've already stapled it shut," the nurse told us. Her name tag read "Alison" and she looked about Nicole's age. She had matching tattoos on both of her arms---some kind of script writing in blue that I couldn't quite make out, and matching roses. I could see the envy in Nicole's eyes as she admired the artistry in ink. To me, raised in another era, it just looked cheap, especially on a young woman. In my day, the only people sporting tattoos were old sailors, with the emphasis on OLD.

Sigh. I am so behind the times. I can't for the life of me fathom why people intentionally put holes in their jeans.

And.....Now I'm starting to sound like my mother.

"Is she in any pain?" I asked Alison, as Mom beamed happily at three of her five granddaughters.

"No, we did a localized pain killer similar to novocaine," Alison said. "I don't think she'll feel anything even after it wears off. We had to use staples because her skin is so thin that it wouldn't take stitches. The nurse at Sunset Place can take the staples out in a few days and give her some Tylenol if she needs it. Once the doctor has seen her, your mom can probably go home."

"That'll be nice," Mom chirped. "No offense, Sweetie. Everyone here is so nice. But I'm a little tired now and want to be in my own bed. Where is my car? Did I leave it out front? I'm ready to drive home."

Allison explained that a little confusion was normal after a trauma. She assured us that standard procedure was to transport her back to Sunset Place in a private service ambulance. It wasn't advisable for us to transport her in one of our cars.

"Don't worry, her Medicare will cover the cost," she told us.

Nicole gently brushed Mom's hair as her sisters kissed Grandma goodbye and headed off to work and school. There really was no point in their staying, now that the crisis was apparently over.

"Bye, Sweetie. Bye, Sweetie," Mom said to both of them as she blew them fond kisses. I could tell she had no idea who they were, but she had enjoyed every minute of their company.

"Do you know who they were?" Gary asked Mom.

"Who?" Mom asked.

"The girls who were just here to see you," my brother said.

"Were they nurses?" Mom guessed. "They were awfully nice. They treated me real well."

"Do you know who I am?" Gary asked her.

Mom thought for a moment, not wanting to show that she had no clue, because she didn't want anyone to know that she couldn't remember, and she certainly didn't want to hurt anyone's feelings. She knew he looked familiar. Suddenly the light went on.

"My brother," she declared, triumphant. "I'd know you anywhere."

Gary and I exchanged glances.

"How about me, Lois?" Ed asked. "Who am I?"

Mom searched deep into her memory bank and came up empty. She decided to improvise.

"Are you my boyfriend?" she asked shyly.

"That's right," Ed told her.

"He's Cary Grant," Gary joked. He loved to confuse her; for some reason he thought it was funny, but somehow she always seemed to enjoy playing along.

"Really? I thought Cary Grant already had a wife; several, as a matter of fact," Mom said, her eyes narrowing with suspicion. No one could pull the wool over her eyes.

"You'll be lucky number seven," my crazy brother informed her. I gave him my usual CEASE AND DESIST sign. He usually ignored it, as he did now.

Mom made a face, suddenly realizing it was a joke.

"Ah, go on," she said, waving dismissively. "He's not Cary Grant. And he's not my boyfriend, either."

"So who is your boyfriend, Mom?" I asked, expecting to hear "Jack," my Dad's name, come from her lips without hesitation.

"Ray, I think," she said, frowning in concentration, naming her boyfriend before Dad. Yikes. I hoped Dad wasn't listening from Heaven.

At that moment, the doctor entered the room, holding a chart. He had the middle-aged, all business bustle as he introduced himself, probably for the 20th time that morning.

"I'm Dr. Raymond," he announced to no one in particular as he casually glanced around the room. "Are you her family?"

Well, we're not her fan entourage, I thought, suppressing a chuckle.

221

"Yes, Doctor," I told him. "I'm her daughter and POA, this is my brother, these are our spouses, and that is my niece, Mom's granddaughter."

"Oh, that's who she is," Mom said. "I thought she was my nurse."

Dr. Raymond said, "Your mother had a urinary tract infection, which often causes confusion and imbalance. She is very frail, but luckily there were no broken bones or concussion.

"Are you my boyfriend, Ray?" Mom asked him, flashing her most coquettish smile.

"I am for the moment, I guess, young lady," he said, patting her hand and smiling.

Mom blushed bright pink with pleasure, unless that was just a reaction to medication.

"Are you ready to go home?" he asked Mom.

"With YOU?" she asked, alarmed, blushing deep crimson. "I'm not that kind of a girl, you must know, Ray."

I signed the release papers as Nicole changed Mom back into her flannel nightgown, robe, and slippers for the ambulance ride back to Sunset Place. Within minutes, two burly young men appeared with a gurney, transferred Mom onto it, and told us we could meet them back at Sunset Place.

"Are you taking me to the hospital?" Mom asked them.

"Mom, you ARE in the hospital," I assured her. "These young men are taking you home."

"Back to Jakes Prairie?" Mom said. "Do Mom and Pop know I'm coming?"

"You'll be home soon, and back in your bed," I told her.

"Goody," she nodded, grinning.

Chapter Twenty-four

"Is he your boyfriend, or is he my boyfriend?"

September 21, 2018

Mom's head wound healed gradually, with no residual complications except for another inch-long scar in the scalp on the back of her head. She seemed oblivious to it, and didn't mind when Head Nurse Nancy checked it and measured it every day.

But, as it often happens, the fall accelerated her mental decline. She still waved to me when I walked through the main door, and greeted me with joy, but I don't think she always knew who I was. She introduced me to the other ladies at the table, or to Sharonda and the other attendants; sometimes I was her daughter, but other times I was her mother, sometimes her sister, and once I was even her husband. At least, she realized we somehow had a close connection.

She usually knew Gary, and occasionally she recognized Ed, but the rest of the family faded out of her memory. She enjoyed the granddaughters' infrequent visits, as well as occasional visits from one of her neighbors, but she had no idea who they were, and never remembered from one day to the next that they had been there.

Things started disappearing from her room, or from her person. First, I noticed that one hearing aid was missing. I asked Sharonda, who said she couldn't find it while dressing Mom that morning.

" I looked all over for it, especially in the covers, or behind the bed, but just couldn't find it," she told me. "I can't imagine where it could have gone, unless she somehow flushed it down the toilet."

After lunch, I wheeled Mom down to her room and helped her into bed. I searched the room the best I could as Mom slept, but it just wasn't there. I did find a small notebook labeled BILL on her end table, next to her chair. Curious, and wondering whether it pertained to Mom at all, I opened it to one page.

There, in careful engineer's drawing, was a diagram of the hallway and exit next to Mom's room. Apparently Bill had drawn his escape route. I closed the book and put it in my pocket, to turn in to Nancy on my way out.

We never did find the missing hearing aid. The following week, the other hearing aid disappeared. This was more serious, because it was the one that worked best. Unless we found it, I would be "talking" to Mom by writing down my words for her to read.

Which was what we did from that point on. Mom was virtually deaf without them, but I didn't see any reason to bring the audiologist back to measure her for replacements. That process had frightened her, and the results were negligible. Sharonda said that the hearing aids hadn't done much good lately, and Mom was pretty good at reading lips, so we all adjusted to the loss of the hearing aids.

Once at lunch, I noticed one of Mom's rings was missing. We had her valuable rings safely stored in our safe deposit box, because we know things tend to disappear in nursing home settings. Mom's fingers had become so thin that her rings just slid off her hand. I told Sharonda about the missing ring, and she said she'd keep an eye out for it.

Six months later, at lunch one day, I noticed that Mom was wearing the no-longer-missing ring. To this day, we have no idea where it had been for half a year, but it was back on her finger. Sharonda suggested I take it home before it could disappear again. She placed it in a small plastic bag for me.

It had very little monetary value, but had been a gift from my brother Ken, and had meant a lot to her. I left her high school class ring on her finger, and her wedding ring. I didn't have the heart to take them from her. She had worn the first one since 1937 and the other two since 1946. They were worn thin, and the tiny diamond had long since been lost from her engagement ring, but I couldn't imagine her fingers without them.

At one point, her glasses disappeared. The entire staff searched and searched, but to no avail. Three weeks later, her granddaughters Nicole and Kelly visited Mom and took pictures of her, grinning broadly, sporting an oversized pair of black rimmed glasses.

"Where on earth did she get those?" I asked them.

"We have no idea," Kelly replied. "But they won't hurt her eyes. They have no lenses."

A month later, Mom was wearing her own glasses again.

"They just showed up somehow," Sharonda said.

Mom's memory loss continued to accelerate, and the upside was I got the happy duty of announcing to her that she had two children, five granddaughters, and (now) five great-grandchildren, over and over again. My grandkids, God bless them, enjoyed visiting Great Grandma when they were in the area. I would give them crayons, markers, and paper ahead of time, and have them draw and label "selfies" for her, which they would present to her with a proud flourish, and Mom would dutifully compliment them on their art work. They would then sing "You Are My Sunshine," to her, and she would perk up and try to sing along, waving her index fingers as a baton to lead the singing.

But as much as we were prepared for her lack of recognition, or her confusion about who was who, the hardest part for me to handle was her lack of memory of Dad, her Jack.

I usually brought labeled photos with me, which she perused with curiosity and interest, and she would sometimes recognize her siblings and parents, but when I showed her a photo of Dad, she would draw a blank.

"Handsome guy," she said. "Who is he?"

That hit me right in the heart.

Several times she would ask curiously, "Was I ever married?"

"Yes, you were, for 56 happy years," I would reply. "Can you guess his name?"

She would struggle with that for a moment, then guess, "Ray?"

Oh, dear. Hope you're not listening, Dad.

I would show her Dad's photo and tell her about Jack, and about their World War II romance by letters.

"I wish I could remember," she would say with a sigh.

"It's okay, Mom," I would assure her. "You're allowed to forget from time to time."

She became quite a flirt at Sunset Place, which surprised me.

After Grace left to become a bank teller, the turnover increased at Sunset Place, especially in the memory care unit. Sometimes I would learn a caregiver's name and get to know them, only to find them gone on my next visit. Nurse Nancy left at the beginning of the year, replaced by Adrienne, who didn't seem quite as sharp as Nancy, but far surpassed her in the empathy and compassion department.

"I just love Lois," Adrienne told me, over and over. "She is so sweet and grateful for everything we do for her, except give her a shower. She fights us over that."

I assured Adrienne this was not news to me, and again suggested the facility consider getting a walk-in-tub for those who don't like showers. She said she would pass the idea along, but I shouldn't hold my breath.

Another new staff member was DeShaun, a tall, handsome young man with soulful dark eyes and a kind manner. Mom developed a crush on him from his first day on the job.

"Is he my boyfriend?" Mom whispered, giggling, to me one day at lunch, while she waved to him and blushed bright pink.

He wiggled his fingers back at her and grinned. I secretly hoped it was all very innocent, but a twinge of worry flitted briefly across my brain. Ashamed at what I was thinking, I nevertheless decided to keep a quiet eye on the situation. Mom was totally incapable of defending herself, or even of asking for help. It was scary to think of her as completely vulnerable.

Over time, DeShaun and Mom developed a teasing friendship. I came to the conclusion that Mom's crush on him was very innocent, and was actually perking her up. She became more aware of her appearance, and watched for him as he bustled around the dining room. They traded mock insults back and forth, and Mom thoroughly enjoyed herself. I got a glimpse of the flirty young girl she had been.

One day Mom pointed to DeShaun and asked me, "Is he your boyfriend?"

"No, Mom, I'm happily married."

"You are?" she asked, incredulously. "How long has that been going on?"

"Forty-seven years," I replied.

"And I never met him?" she accused me, her eyes narrowing.

"No, you've known him the whole time." I showed her a photo of Ed.

"He does look familiar," she told me. "Well, good for you. Was I ever married?"

"I sure hope so," I replied, chuckling. So I pulled out the family photos and went over them with her, again.

She was pleased to discover that she had five granddaughters and five great-grandchildren. I showed her both of my daughters with their husbands and children, and Mom's eyes narrowed.

"So your girls have children," she said. "Are they married? I sure hope they are."

I assured her that both girls were happily married.

"Well, that's good," she said. "At least you raised them right. You never know about young people these days. In my day, having children without a husband was unthinkable."

All I could do was agree with her.

Mom's favorite caregiver was Sharonda, who seemed born to the special calling of working with elderly people. Her patience knew no bounds. During lunch one day, I asked her how she could keep her frustrations in check as she cared for people who were sometimes violent and seldom co-operative.

"Having patients like Lois helps a lot," Sharonda said. "She is so sweet, and she appreciates everything we do. It's always sad to watch them deteriorate and get so confused, but we are helping them ease into their final journey Home."

"You are such a blessing to Mom," I told her.

"I feel closer to her than I do to my own mother," Sharonda admitted. "I'm going to need bereavement leave when she passes. I feel like one of her family."

"You are, Sharonda, in a very special way."

Mom's confusion continued to escalate. She was still rational, but the light was fading from her eyes, and she lost interest in the everyday society of Sunset Place. She no longer watched the door, and no longer anticipated what the day's dessert was. She seemed oblivious to TV shows she used to enjoy, and no longer commented on the weather outside the window. She was starting to lose her interest in life.

When she stopped flirting with DeShaun, I knew it was a sign. I went to see Adrienne. It was time to bring in Hospice.

Chapter Twenty-five

October 28, 2018

"Everyone is so nice to me."

Gary and Pattie, and Ed and I met with Hospice representatives in a small conference room at Sunset Place in late October. We all agreed that it was probably time to involve them in Mom's care. Adrienne had already contacted them at our request.

Mary Beth was in her 50s, a large lady with grey hair and kind eyes. Her photo ID tag read Hospice Director of Client Services. I noticed she wore a small gold crucifix around her neck.

Accompanying her were two other women, one in her forties and another in her 30s, guessing. They wore matching navy blue shirts with HOSPICE OF THE WESTERN RESERVE embroidered on the breast pocket. The introduced themselves as Cheryl and Joanna.

"We have reviewed your mom's file with our staff doctor, with the history of her symptoms and treatment," Mary Beth began. "She has all the symptoms of advanced Alzheimer's, and definitely qualifies for our services."

Gary and I exchanged looks.

"Alzheimer's?" I asked. "We thought Mom has dementia. Her mother and brother both had Alzheimer's, but Mom never seemed irrational like

232

they were. She just seemed to have serious memory loss."

"Our staff doctor diagnosed Alzheimer's, definitely," Mary Beth insisted gently, with a nod. Cheryl and Joanna nodded in unison, concurring.

Mary Beth explained that there are many different types of Alzheimer's, and Mom's type was fairly common.

She then handed us manuals and pointed out her attached business card, telling us we could reach her on her cell phone 24/7.

"Our mission is to work with Lois and your entire family, every step of the way," she told us. "And when the time comes, and her journey takes her on to the next step, we will handle all the details and help your family with whatever you need. We will follow you with bereavement services as long as you need us."

Her warm, reassuring voice made my face start to leak. It would be great to have someone else helping with all the steps to come—someone who knew how to help us make the right decisions along the way.

"That's been the hard part," I told her. "We want to do what is best for Mom, of course, but it's been years since Dad passed and we made decisions for him. Sometimes it's hard to know the right thing to do. We've always tried to determine what Dad would want us to do. It's good to have help from people who deal with this all the time. We really appreciate the help."

Mary Beth explained that her team would assess Mom's needs and devise a specific game plan for her. Cheryl's job was devising the plan, and Joanna would be Mom's assigned caregiver.

"I typically visit all the clients we have here at Sunset Place at least twice a week, more if needed," Joanna explained. "I will do a physical exam, treat any wounds, weigh her, and find out whether she is eating and is hydrated. I make sure she is comfortable and in no pain. I will sit with her, read to her, do puzzles with her, or anything that makes her happy."

Mary Beth explained that Mom would be given medicines only to keep her comfortable, not to hinder the natural progression of her condition. We had already signed the Do Not Resuscitate order years ago, at Mom's own request, when she gave me power of attorney. She explained to us the specifics of what that meant.

She asked us several questions, including what funeral home we would be using. I was taken aback.

"Sorry if that startled you," Mary Beth said gently. "But when the time comes, we will handle transport. We need to know where. It saves a lot of confusion and distress when the time comes."

I gave her the name of the local funeral home that had served Mom's family going back three generations. Gary nodded in agreement. Mary Beth strongly recommended that we contact the funeral director as soon as possible to pre-plan the arrangements.

"It will help everyone if you're not faced with a hundred little decisions at the very time you are mourning your mom," she said.

She then asked us to describe Mom's personality, and our relationship with her over the years. We explained that Mom had been a happy, caring, young mother who loved to take care of her kids, husband, and home. She had been an experimental cook, sometimes with great results, and sometimes not so great, but had been an amazing baker.

We had been very happy during the youngest days of our childhood, until Mom had a mental breakdown when I was 12 and Gary was 7. She had suffered from severe depression for more than 30 years, and had made our adolescences almost unbearable. Somehow, we had managed to survive.

Mary Beth nodded, made a few notes, and smiled.

"And now?"

We told her that one good thing about dementia, Alzheimer's, or whatever it was, was that Mom seemed to have forgotten all the bad times—and there were a lot of those—and had become just a sweet little old lady, appreciative of everything anyone did for her.

"In other words, you got the great Mom back that you remembered from your childhood," Mary Beth said.

I hadn't thought about it that way, but that statement took the last shreds of resentment away and lifted a burden I had been carrying around for more than a half century. Remembering how ideal and loving our early childhood had been, my face started leaking in earnest.

Mary Beth gave me several papers to sign as POA, on behalf of Mom. She explained that they would be taking over supervising her care, would keep her in most of her supplies, including adult diapers, and we would still need to continue supplying wipes, personal items, and liquid dietary supplements such as Boost. They would also supply equipment such as reclining wheel chairs and hospital beds.

"About the bed," I said. I explained what her king sized bed meant to her. Mary Beth said she could continue to use it.

Whew. That would be a deal breaker if they insisted on a hospital bed. That is one thing I would never compromise on. Dad would haunt me forever if I let anyone make that change.

That bed was her anchor, her home, her security blanket.

Mom took to Joanna almost as much as she loved Sharonda.

Now, when I visited, Mom would hold my hand and kiss it tenderly. It broke my heart to see how emaciated she had become, but the love in her eyes warmed my heart. Mary Beth was right. I had gotten the loving Mom of my childhood back.

She stopped eating sometime in late October. Joanna told me that was a sign. She ordered Mom's diet changed to pureed food, hoping that if it were easier to eat, Mom might be tempted into an appetite.

Sharonda and DeShaun moved Mom to the feeding table, where the worst-off residents sat and were hand fed. It was sad to see that move, because she was sitting with Dorothy, who chanted constantly when she was awake, but who slept through most meals, uninterested in food. Everyone understood that Dorothy would not be with us much longer.

Then there was Ernie, who bent over double in his wheel chair, oblivious to just about everything. The few times he was awake, he called out for Helen, over and over, but Helen had passed away in 1987. Ernie had been the best wedding cake baker in the county. As a matter of fact, he had made Ed's and my wedding cake back in 1971.

Mom was now the third at the table. Sharonda and DeShaun took turns trying, mostly in vain, to spoon feed all three of them. Mom could still handle the eating process without spilling anything, but she had to be reminded to eat. She would greedily drain her glass of cranberry juice, then bang it on the table in a demand for more. After the third glass, she would fall asleep, her head back on the pillow of her new reclining wheel chair, her mouth open, snoring loudly.

When she woke up, Sharonda would try to feed her a few bites of pureed food.

"Ugh! Baby food!" was Mom's reaction at first. But as the weeks passed, she would permit Sharonda or me to spoon small amounts into her mouth. Usually after three or four bites, she would push the spoon aside and shake her head.

"I'm full," she would declare. "I don't want any more."

Sharonda was very good at cajoling Mom to drink a few sips of Boost or some other liquid supplement, or to eat a few spoonfuls of pudding or ice cream. Mom shrank to 84 pounds of skin and bones. Worse, she also developed a bed sore from spending so much time sleeping.

Joanna noticed it first, and called me immediately. Apparently, a bed sore---even a tiny one---is very serious. Joanna said it was the size of a dime, and right on Mom's tail bone.

"She seemed uncomfortable when she was sitting, so I examined her," Joanna told me. "I showed it to Adrienne, who said she had just checked Lois after her shower yesterday and didn't see it. I find that hard to believe, but okay. I put a dressing on it, and will check it every time I'm here."

The bed sore took forever to heal. Joanna gave me regular reports, and seemed pleased that it didn't get any larger. It shrank very slowly over the next few weeks, but never went away entirely.

"It doesn't seem to be bothering her anymore, so that's one good thing," Joanna said. "I'm keeping a close eye on it. If it gets any worse, or I see another one, I'll send her to the hospital for a doctor to treat her."

"They have a doctor on staff at Sunset Place," I told Joanna. "He signs reports all the time. I see the signatures. When we brought Mom there, they assured me that a staff doctor would examine her regularly."

Joanna snorted.

"Maybe that's what they told you, but the doctor on their staff never really sees the residents," she said. "He's only there to sign orders and prescriptions, and to pronounce them when they pass. The actual medical work is done by the nurse practitioner. Most of the facilities I work with do it that way."

"That doesn't seem right," I said. "What happens if it's something more serious than the nurse can handle?"

"That's when they call an ambulance to take them to the hospital," Joanna said. "They worry about liability, so that's their standard procedure. That way they've done their due diligence."

"No wonder I've never met him, despite my requests, all this time," I said.

"It's how most of them operate. An actual doctor, on staff, is too expensive. This way they have him on retainer to do the staff the NP can't do."

As time went on, Joanna took over Mom's care more and more. Mom seemed content, and continued to rave about her care, but she still did not want to eat. Sharonda and Joanna tried to change the color of the plate, tempting her with her favorite foods, and rewarding her with candy when she took a bite, but the simple fact was, Mom had lost interest in eating. I wondered how long she could last on a few ounces of cranberry juice and three or four cans of Boost every day.

She even lost interest in M&Ms.

Chapter Twenty-six

"If they belong to you, that means they also belong to me."

November 23, 2018

We celebrated Mom's 99th birthday with a quiet family gathering in the auxiliary dining room. Everyone was there, which was becoming increasingly challenging to arrange. Mom sat at the end of a big table, with Gary next to her and me at the opposite end. Gary's wife Pattie, my husband Ed, Gary's daughter Nicole and her boyfriend Brian, Gary's daughter Kelly and her husband Ryan, Gary's daughter Jessie and her boyfriend Erik, Ed's and my daughter Megan, her husband Matt, their daughters Bridget, Clare and Norah, Ed's and my daughter Katie and her husband David, and their little boys, Jack and Luke.

Sharonda reluctantly joined us, at Mom's request.

"She's like a daughter to me," Mom announced. "She's so good to me."

We welcomed Sharonda, who told us she could only join us for a few minutes.

Although we all realized that this was very likely Mom's last birthday, we made it as festive as possible. We also knew she tired easily, so we made it brief. Each of the little ones got a balloon, and

Nicole put the sparkly plastic birthday tiara on the birthday girl.

"How old are you, Mom?" Pattie asked her.

Mom glanced cautiously around the table and thought for a moment.

"Well, I guess I must be close to a hundred," she speculated.

"That's right, Lois!" Ed said. "You're 99 today!"

"Well, for cryin' out loud," Mom observed. "I never thought I'd live to be this old. And I want you all to know, I do not want to live to be 100."

We all looked at each other in disbelief. What elderly person ever announced that they didn't want to be 100?

We all realized at that moment that she was going to get her wish. Mom always called the shots, and almost always got her way.

The little ones, oblivious to the conversation, called out in unison, "HAPPY BIRTHDAY, GREAT GRANDMA!" and sang to her the song they had been practicing for weeks:

You are my sunshine, my only sunshine

You make me happy when skies are grey

You'll never know, Dear, how much I love you

Please don't take my sunshine away

242

The second time around, Mom recognized the song, which her mother had sung to her, and Mom had sung to all of us, beginning with me, her first child, to her granddaughters, all the way down to the great-grandkids.

She tried to sing along with them, but it came out in an unrecognizable croak. We pretended not to notice, and all of us chimed in as she led us with a weak wave of her hand and a blinding smile.

Megan set the birthday cake in front of Mom, with one small lighted candle.

"Why? Am I one?" Mom asked.

"If we put all 99 on it, we'd have to get a much bigger cake," Gary joked.

"And it would probably set off the smoke alarms," Ed added.

Mom tried four times to blow the little candle out, but her aim was off and her breathing was weak. When she finally succeeded, everyone applauded with enthusiasm. And, following family tradition, she made the first cut.

But when Nicole tried to feed a bite of cake to her, Mom said, "I'm really full. I don't want any."

Nicole cajoled her into taking a bite. Then Mom took the fork from her and took a few bites on her own.

"Butter cream frosting has always been my favorite," she said. "It's the best." With her fork, she scooped a big bite of frosting and plopped it into her mouth with a look of satisfaction.

As she ate, each of the kids walked up to her, one by one, introduced themselves, and kissed her on the cheek. Katie introduced her two boys to Mom again, and Mom perked up when she heard that one of them was named Jack.

"For my Jack?" Mom marveled. "He would be so pleased."

My face started leaking, as Mom remembered Dad, without prompting, for the first time in months.

Then Mom glanced around the table, and the light came on in her eyes.

"Wait a minute!" she exclaimed, pointing at me.

"If they all belong to YOU, that means they all belong to ME!" she said, triumph in her voice. "Well, I'll be darned. Isn't that something?"

The faces of all the other adults started leaking too. The little ones looked at us, a bit confused.

"We're not sad, kids," I assured them. "We're just very happy."

"Happy Birfday TO YOU, happy birfday TO YOU!" yelled little Luke, two years old, in a squeaky singsong voice. Drat! I should have recorded it.

Mom smiled, and, just as quickly as it came, the light faded again.

"I'm really very tired now," she announced. "Can you take me to bed? I need a little nap."

Sharonda wheeled her down the hall, with our whole family parading behind. When Mom was ensconced in her big bed and covered with her photo blanket, it was time for all of us to go. Tears rolled down Katie's cheeks---as the granddaughter who lived out of state, 600 miles away, she realized she was probably seeing her grandma alive for the last time.

I put my arm around Katie and gave her a reassuring hug.

"Grandma has lived a very long life, but now she's tired," I said softly, my voice faltering. "You gave her a great gift today, bringing the kids to see her on her birthday. She gave us an even better gift today. She remembered Grandpa, and she remembered we are her family. That means so much, don't you think?"

Chapter Twenty-seven

"So it's a happy ending. Wonderful."

February 10, 2019

Sunday, as was my custom, I went to see Mom after church. Usually the timing coincided perfectly with her lunch, but this Sunday, when I was buzzed into the memory unit, no waves, Yoo Hoos, or For Cryin' Out Louds greeted me. I checked around both dining rooms, to no avail.

Finally I spotted DeShaun, who came over to me, a solemn, sympathetic expression on his face. He looked near tears.

"We couldn't get her up, either for breakfast or lunch," he told me. "She made it very clear that she had no intention of leaving her bed today. We tried everything, but she wouldn't budge."

"Yes, she can be very stubborn, as you know only too well," I told him.

He walked with me down the hall and unlocked her door for me.

"Maybe she'll listen to you," he said.

"That would be a first," I said with a chuckle. "She's never listened to me before. Mom always calls her own shots."

I glanced across the room to the big bed, and, covered by her picture quilt, there was a tiny, Mom-shaped lump on what had always been her side of the bed for more than a half century. Long after Dad passed, 17 years ago, she still saved his side of the bed for his return.

I stood there, watching Mom's chest move up and down, ever so slightly. She smiled in her sleep, and seemed totally at peace.

I picked up a well worn book on her nightstand, surprised to recognize "Love Always," the book of Dad's World War II letters to her, that I'd had published the year before. Someone had obviously been reading it regularly, based on the worn cover. A bookmark held the place. I was startled at the realization that either someone was reading it to her, or she was reading it herself, enjoying the story but oblivious to the fact that the book was about her romance with Dad 75 years ago.

Mom stirred a little and made a slight mewing sound as she turned toward me and opened her eyes.

"Well, for cryin' out loud," she said with a grin. "What are you doing here? How did you find me?"

"I came to check on you," I told her, kissing her cheek. "They told me you wanted to stay in bed today. Are you being lazy, or are you sick?"

She grabbed my hand and kissed it tenderly.

"Sit down," she said. "I want to talk to you."

I took a seat in a folding chair, inches away from the bed. I was surprised that she could hear me.

Mom blinked her eyes awake and sighed.

"I keep seeing people in my head," she said. "Mom, Pop, Ken, Marty, Opal, Amy, Buell---they're all there."

I nodded.

"Jack too," I said gently, as my face started leaking.

"Jack's here?" she asked, struggling to sit up. She sounded delighted and joyful with anticipation, like a child on Christmas Eve waiting for Santa.

"Yes, Mom, he's there too. He's close by, waiting for you. He's been waiting a long time."

"Me too."

"Mom, you know why those people are there, don't you?" I ventured. "You once told me about your own Dad describing it as like a train station, with everyone waiting for him."

Mom nodded, and sighed. She knew. She remembered.

"So when you see the light, go to it," I told her softly, no longer able to trust my shaky voice. "They'll all be there waiting, Jack especially. He'll be at the front of the line, to welcome you."

She nodded again, then beamed, her face shining with joy.

"So it's to be a happy ending," she whispered.

My face leaking profusely by now, I could only nod. She got it.

"Wonderful," she said.

We held hands for a few minutes, and she kissed mine from time to time.

"Now, I'm tired. You go on home. I want to take a little nap now. Don't worry. I'll be fine."

I reluctantly obeyed. Mom deserved to call the shots, as she always had. I kissed her and turned to go.

As I glanced back at her one more time, she waved and called softly, "You're a good girl."

I lost it entirely then. Sharonda was waiting for me in hall. She didn't have to say anything as she wrapped her arms around me and we sobbed together.

"It won't be long now," she whispered. "The angels are gathering." I told her what Mom had described. She nodded, having seen similar moments countless times before.

"You go on home now, Honey," Sharonda said. "I'll let you know when it changes. Get yourself some rest. You're gonna need it."

Joanna called me twice a day, and said that Mom was resting comfortably, sleeping most of the time.

"There's really nothing you can do for her right now," she said. "She's never fully conscious, but she is very peaceful. She doesn't seem to be aware of us as we sit with her. There is no reason at this point for you to be here at the moment. We'll call you when there's a change."

"We had a wonderful visit together on Sunday," I told her. "Not only could she hear every word I said, her mind was clear. She knows where she's going."

"I suggest you hold onto that great memory," Joanna said. "There is really no reason for you to come until we see the sign. I think we should just let her sleep in the meantime. I'll call you as soon as there is a change."

The call I expected, yet dreaded, came late Tuesday afternoon. As soon as my caller ID read HOSPICE, I knew.

"It's time," Joanna said simply. "I'll sit with her until you all can get here, but don't be long."

I told Ed, who quickly gathered both of our coats, then called Gary and Pattie, and our two girls. Gary said quietly, "Okay. I'll let my three know and we'll all head over there."

"We're on our way," I told him.

When Ed and I arrived at Sunset Place, Gary and Pattie were already there. Nicole and Jessie were sitting on the bed with Mom, who was flailing her shoulders in her sleep and moaning softly.

250

"Is she in any pain?" Gary asked Joanna.

"No, not at all," she responded. "She is walking toward the light. She's trying to run."

Darn my leaky face. I took out a Kleenex, wiped the drops from my eyes, and took a seat in a folding chair next to the bed. Nicole and Jessie were actively weeping.

Megan, then Katie, called by video, one on Ed's cell, and one on mine. Both were struggling to hold back their tears. The great-grandkids were openly crying.

"I wish we could be there," Megan said.

"Grandma knows you're here with her in spirit," I assured her. "You all were here with her at Christmas, and she really enjoyed that."

Katie said, "Play some of her favorite music on Youtube. She'll like that."

The little ones, led by our oldest grandchild, Bridget, sang "You are My Sunshine" one more time. Mom opened her eyes, smiled, and in a croaking voice struggled to sing along.

We took turns on Youtube finding her old favorite Glenn Miller songs, Dad's old favorite "Stardust," and others she had loved. Occasionally she opened her eyes briefly and smiled, then closed them again and resumed her journey.

As the last notes of "Boogie Woogie Bugle Boy of Company B" faded on my phone, Mom suddenly opened her eyes and exclaimed, "Jack!"

251

"That's right, Mom," I said. "He loved that song."

Mom glanced around the room, first at Ed, then me, followed by Gary, Pattie, then Nicole and Jessie.

"Kelly?" Mom asked.

Wow. Mom hadn't remembered Kelly's name in more than a year.

"Kelly's on her way, Mom," I said. "She'll be here in a few minutes."

Mom nodded, then fell back onto her pillow, closed her eyes, and the flailing told us she was heading toward the light again.

Just then, Kelly hurried into the room. When she found a spot on the bed, next to Mom, she sat down and whispered softly, "Grandma, I'm here."

Mom stopped flailing and her eyes fluttered open as Kelly took her hand. Mom pulled her close as Kelly kissed her. Mom smiled, kissed Kelly tenderly on the cheek, and sighed. She fell back onto her pillow, a look of happy contentment filling her face.

She nodded, closed her eyes, and took her last breath. It left her quietly. She was smiling.

"She's gone," sobbed Nicole.

"She's back with Dad now," I said, my tears falling on Mom's closed eyes as I kissed her forehead. "They've been waiting a long time, and now they're finally together again. Kiss Dad for me, Mom."

Joanna bent over her, confirmed that Mom was no longer breathing, and summoned the Hospice doctor who had been waiting in the hallway to come in and officially pronounce her dead.

"Take as long as you want," Joanna told us. "Transport is waiting outside to take her to the funeral home. Whenever you're ready."

She took me aside and pressed something in my hand. It was the well worn copy of "Love Always," the book of Dad's World War II letters to Mom, that I had transcribed and published six months before.

"Lois loved that book," Joanna whispered. "I doubt that she knew it was about her, but she got a lot of pleasure from reading those letters. I would sit and read them to her, but often she just enjoyed reading them herself. See? She kept a bookmark in her place."

One by one, we all took turns saying our final sad goodbyes to Mom. Even though we knew this had been coming for several months, and she had filled her 99 years with countless life experiences, it still seemed unreal that she was gone, after being such a major part of our entire lives.

The next day, all of us met at the Davis Funeral Home in Willoughby, which had held funerals in Mom's family going back to her dad's in 1946. My aunt, grandmother, baby brother Glenn, our brother Ken, and Dad, had all been buried from there. We had spent a lot of time over the years in its main room.

We all agreed that Mom wanted to be cremated, and her ashes scattered where we had put Dad's, on a beautiful hilltop in West Virginia where the family had vacationed every year. Ken's ashes were there, too.

Gary had another suggestion as well.

"Why don't we take some of Mom's ashes back to the site of the old family homestead in Jakes Prairie where she was born?" he asked.

"That's a wonderful idea," I said, mad at myself for not thinking of it.

We discussed memorial services, and everyone agreed that Mom would hate having it during cold, gloomy weather. We settled on mid May, when the sun was (hopefully) shining, the flowers blooming, and the wrens singing.

"Mom would approve of that," I said. "And it will give our girls and the other relatives plenty of time to plan for work schedules and travel."

So on a warm, bright Saturday morning in May, we gathered at the funeral home to celebrate and honor Mom's almost-century of life. It was too early to harvest irises and lilacs from Mom's garden, so we did our best with a spray of spring flowers from the florist a block from her house.

Her ashes, in a plain oak box, sat on a dais that we draped with a brightly colored lei, signifying her trip to Hawaii with Dad. We displayed her photo blanket, high school graduation memorabilia, and wedding photo. My pastor gave a simple yet powerful message that Mom would have approved, as his daughter played our old favorite hymns on the piano. I told of Mom's remarkable century of life. Ed, Katie, and Jessie all told funny stories that had the 50 people in the audience laughing, which would have delighted Mom. Megan sang the family's favorite old hymn, "Softly and Tenderly."

Then Katie stood up and led the five great-grandkids, all dressed in their Easter outfits, to the front of the room, lined them up, from the oldest, Bridget, 11, to 8-year-old Clare, then Norah, 5, and little Jack, 5. She held the youngest, Luke, 2, and led them in one final song:

You are My Sunshine

My only sunshine

You make me happy

When skies are grey

You'll never know, Dear,

How much I love you.

Please don't take my sunshine away.

Afterword

October 4, 2019

To my beloved family----

Now it is my turn to be the official family elder. I have chronicled Grandma's journey and her struggle with dementia, with the very real possibility that someday, hopefully a long time from now, it will be my turn, and you will be taking care of me.

If it does happen, please don't be sad. I've led a wonderful, long life filled with the greatest blessings that our loving God can bestow on His child. He sent me your dad, who has been my life mate and partner for almost a half century (so far). Together we've built a wonderful life together. It hasn't been perfect, but with our mutual love of Jesus at the center of our household, we have been blessed beyond belief.

Our greatest blessings have been the two of you. We did our best to raise you right, as we had been raised. We taught you about the Lord, and we are so grateful that you both listened, learned, and decided to follow His path. You have found wonderful husbands, and built happy and productive lives with them, and, more important, happy homes and amazing families of your own.

If my journey includes the dementia that challenged my grandmother, uncle, and mother, please be patient with me and remember what I have been to you over your lifetime, not what I became. Make good decisions for me, but don't sacrifice your own lives and families in the process.

Keep the good memories alive with your kids, my beloved grandchildren. Show them pictures and tell them stories of happy times together. Let them understand that I still, and will always, love them very much.

And always---always---follow the Lord, and teach your children to as well.

"Train up a child in the way he should go, and when he is old, he will not part from it." Proverbs 22:6.

And through it all, remember the love I have for you, and always will.   Love, Mom

Appendix

Tips and Suggestions for Caregivers:

I am not an attorney, or by any means an expert when it comes to eldercare, but I want to share with you some suggestions, based on what worked for us, and what didn't.

1. As soon as you expect that a loved one is showing signs of dementia or Alzheimer's, discuss with them the need to assign a durable Power of Attorney, a health care Power of Attorney, advanced directives such as a Do Not Resuscitate order, Living Will, and an up to date will. It is important to do this while the person is mentally competent, otherwise someone may challenge it in court. I recommend having a licensed attorney prepare the documents and file them with the county of residence.

2. Keep copies of the documents in your glove compartment, along with your loved one's health insurance information. Keep another set on file, possibly in a safe deposit box, and give sets to other family members if possible.

3. Research care options before the need to make decisions.

4. Each situation is unique. As much as possible, talk to your loved one about his or her wishes, so when

the time comes, you will do what you think they would want.

5. Spend as much time as possible with your loved one, so you can recognize their symptoms as they accelerate. You will never regret spending time with them. No one ever says, "I spent too much time with my Mom."

6. De-clutter their living area gradually, removing items that can hurt them such as weapons, knives, old medicines, and harmful chemicals. Remove scatter rugs. Install railings and handles wherever possible.

7. Check with your local Department on Aging for services they offer, such as Meals on Wheels, large item disposal, or consultants that can help with safety and security issues. Many agencies have programs such as day care, respite care, or other services.

8. Understand that your loved one is still your parent, spouse, or friend. Be calm and supporting. Be patient with them. They may be confused and even frightened from time to time. Sympathize with their situation.

9. Never argue, cajole, criticize, or correct them. It will only frustrate and upset them, and they are likely to forget the discussion in a short time. They cannot learn and retain information.

10. Use distraction. Change the subject. Show them something pleasant, give them something they like to

eat, find a familiar program on TV, or play their favorite music.

11. Keep in mind that you are their reality, and their emotional anchor now. As frustrating as that can be, it's your responsibility to make good decisions for them.

12. Realize that you may have to hear the same story, or answer the same question, or have the same conversation over and over again. Their mind recycles, and they don't realize that. They can't control it. Just listen and respond.

13. Share photos with them from their childhood, but don't press them to remember. They might remember one day, but not the next. Enjoy the times when they are clear, but discontinue if they get frustrated or upset.

14. Safety is the priority. Anticipate things in their home that can be dangerous to them (such as putting metal in the microwave or running water in a plugged sink.)

15. Don't try to do this on your own. Enlist help, from professionals if possible. They can determine when the loved one can no longer live at home.

16. Make sure their bills are paid, they do not receive confusing mail, their clothes and body are clean, their toenails trimmed, their glasses and hearing aids functioning, and all the little details taken care of.

17. If possible, rely on family members to work together as a committee on your loved one's behalf.

18. Although your loved one may be frightened of being placed in a facility, at some point it will probably become necessary, to protect them from harm. Moving them can be emotionally painful, but caring professionals are trained in helping them adapt to their new situation. Soon, it will become home to them.

19. Some people are "sundowners," who have great emotional difficulty in the evenings. Talk to a professional about how best to deal with it.

20. If your loved one becomes belligerent, they can be a danger to themselves and to others. Time to get professional help for them.

21. Find whatever makes them happy, or at least contented. Music is a great tool; no matter how the disease progresses, most people still remember their favorite music.

22. Maintain a positive attitude, for their sake. If you are caring for a parent, remember that once you were helpless and relying on them for everything. Now it's their turn.

23. Find time for yourself so you don't burn out. You are no good to anyone if you are frazzled.

24. Lean on your faith, on family, on friends, on your support system. Try to keep your sense of humor.

25. Bring in Hospice when the time comes.

26. Good luck! We've all been there. You are not alone. This is part of life.

Made in the USA
Columbia, SC
13 January 2020